THE WOMAN
THEY CALLED
RAWHIDE

THE WOMAN
THEY CALLED
RAWHIDE

N. PEARL SENECAL

THE WOMAN THEY CALLED RAWHIDE

Published by N. Pearl Senecal, New Hazelton, Canada

ISBN: Paperback: 0-978-1-9990818-0-5
        eBook: 0-978-1-9990818-1-2

Publication assistance and digital printing in Canada by

PUBLISHING
PageMaster.ca

DEDICATION

This book is dedicated to a very loving person, my husband, Lu; my family and friends who have encouraged me, and all those who change lives with their unconditional love.

Thank you to my granddaughter, Chasidy, for making this book possible.

CONTENTS

FOREWARD

Hoping to escape the increasing political unrest in the Ukraine, numbers of Ukrainian peasants emigrated to Canada during the early 1900's, hoping to find land and a place to farm in peace. Among the number that came later, most were Displaced Persons, people whose homes and lands had been confiscated. They had nowhere else to go but Canada. These were the "DPs"

There was no open arm of welcome when they arrived. Fortunately for many settled in block settlements so there was the support of language and culture. These they were spared some of the mockery and hostility that was there in full force in other communities. The immigrants came with nothing but the skills to survive. Dugout homes, or pit homes called burdei or zemliansky were erected for shelter.

During World War One, thousands were sent to camps as "Enemy Aliens," which only increased the difficulties they already faced.

For many there was deep grief. The peasant families that stayed in the old country were starved by the Stalinist Government when soldiers were sent to take all the grain and foodstuffs and sealed the areas, so the peasants could not escape. There are no accurate statistics, but between three million and ten million peasants perished. The rest of the world knew little of this forced starvation. It was only later that the full horror of this government planned genocide was known. The newcomers to Canada knew the situation was bad in the old country. They feared for the lives of the loved ones they left behind but even they did not know the full extent of the famine.

When the Nazi Regime came to power the people at first welcomed them as a way to be freed from Stalin. However, the Nazis murdered at least another four million Ukrainians and Jews and sent others to slave labor camps where untold numbers died.

After coming to Canada not all Ukrainians settled in block groups. For single families that settled in an already established community, life was extremely difficult at times. These were the "Bohunks" that survived in dugout homes, scorned and sometimes hurt by neighbors. They had no cultural support and lived life very much on the edge of society. Some single-family settlers were from Russia and were usually more marginalized and often called "Commies."

The children often went to school dressed in the poorest clothing. At best these children were subjected to a great deal of ridicule and lack of inclusion. At worst they were physically abused, many times by teachers as well as their fellow students.

This story takes place in a farming community and is based on the real stories of survival of some of those, "unwanted and unwelcomed" Russian and Ukrainian families and the powerful woman who you will read about in this story.

Names and places have been changed and somewhat fictionalized to protect the privacy of the descendants of these pioneers

PROLOGUE

There are people you meet that remain in the memory forever. Rawhide was one of those unforgettable ones. Sometimes I think back about the years long past, and in my memory I can still see her smile and hear her soft, gentle voice

She was wheeling him down the sidewalk by the nursing home when I first saw her. Her blue suit complimented her slender, yet curvy body and contrasted beautifully with the mass of silver curls done in an up-sweep. Her soft golden complexion had only the wrinkles of one who smiled a great deal. She was no longer young, but she was still beautiful, perhaps in the same way that autumn can be just as beautiful as summer.

There was something about her that went beyond her physical beauty. There was something intangible about her expression. Was it that she had found complete peace with her life? Was it her deep love for this man? I found myself wondering if hers was the face of an angel. Even after all these years when I try to picture how an angel would look, I see only the face of Rawhide.

The wheel chair held the most marred and scarred human I had ever seen. His face, or what was left of his face, was twisted into thick, ugly, lumpy scars. On the left side he had no ear, and his eye looked out from a hole that had a lumpy eyelid that did not move in unison with the other lid. His lips were thickened by scar tissue, and where his nose should have been were two gaping nostrils. Thick tufts of white hair grew on his head between scars, making his appearance even more grotesque. The right side of his face was also badly scarred, but his eye and ear had escaped better than the left. His right arm hung limply by his side and his right side was propped with pillows to hold him in a more upright position.

The shock I felt at that first sight of his face made me quickly turn away. I couldn't bear the sight of his deformities. The beautiful woman carried herself like royalty. The man looked like a seriously deformed gnome.

I had a thousand questions for the Matron as I signed in to begin my shift. My biggest question was, "Who are they?"

"This gentleman is our new resident. The lady is his wife; a retired lawyer whose only name, it seems, is Rawhide". She picked up his chart and handed it to me. "He is your charge for the rest of the week while you are on duty. They lived on a farm until recently. He has had a stroke, so she decided to purchase a home here in the city where there is better access to rehabilitation. He will be here until she is finished moving. She also needs to arrange for an assistant to help her in their home as the heavy lifting is too much for her. She thinks he will only be here for a month until everything is ready."

The chart told me little except that he was a pleasant and co-operative man. His wife would provide much of his daytime care, but she needed some assistance. He had no allergies. She had signed her name as 'Rawhide". Rawhide made me think of something crude and rough. Something covered with coarse hair. If this was her name it in no way fitted this elegant lady. There had to be a story here.

I filled the water pitcher and went down to their room to meet them. It was easy to see in the way they interacted with each other that there was a lot of love here. Before she left for the night, she tenderly massaged his feet and back, then make sure he had enough blankets to keep him comfortable through the night. As I walked past their room, I heard her say, "I will never stop loving you. Even when I am home resting tonight you need to know that I am thinking of you." He reached for her hand with his one good hand and held it for a moment. I have no idea what he said, but she leaned over and kissed his forehead, then hurried away with tears in her eyes.

The weeks flew by. I got to know them a little before he left the Nursing Home. In spite of his partial paralysis and the difficulties it made for him, I found him to be a patient and kind individual. My opinion of her only increased as a friendship developed between us. One afternoon I found the courage to ask her if she would share the story of their life. She smiled, a far away look in her eyes. She stood looking out the window for a long time. "Our story is a love story", she finally responded. "But it is not some sweet, romantic tale. I am not sure I am ready to share it, or if I even should". She gave my arm a little squeeze and turned away from me.

****

I got the call a year later. It was Rawhide, her voice quivered as she spoke. "My husband passed away last night. The funeral is next Thursday. I hope you can be there. You were so caring of us when we were in the Nursing Home. It would mean the world to me if you could come."

I went. She asked me to stay after the other guests were gone. I did. It was obvious she grieved deeply for her life companion, yet even in her sorrow she exuded strength. Beyond that strength there was that elusive something about her that drew me to her. I could not name it, yet it was there. It made me wonder if she was named Rawhide because of a powerful personality, or was there another reason?

After the last guest left, she led me to the cozy family room where we both sank wearily into soft reclining chairs. She sat silent for some time, staring into the fire flickering in her fireplace. At last she rose and brought me an album of pictures. "Take this home and look at them. I won't tell you anything about the pictures now, but I have decided to tell you my story, and as I tell the story you will learn who the people in the pictures are."

"I know you are on vacation right now," she continued. "I have a cabin in the mountains where I love to go. If you could arrange to spend a week there with me, I will tell you my story -if you still want me to."

Of course, I wanted to hear that story! We made plans; we left three days later.

The cabin was comfortable but rustic. She obviously was a wealthy lady and I admit I was surprised at the humility of the place. I had been expecting a lodge-worthy cabin. I think my face showed my puzzlement. "I want it this way," she said. "I was a very poor girl and sometimes it feels good to go back and touch my beginnings again. It keeps me grounded!" She smiled. "My mother would have thought she was a Princess if her home had been even half this good. Now grab your bag. Your room is at the back of the cabin. The washroom is that little log house at the end of the path. You passed it when you

drove in here. Be sure you watch for bears when you go out there!"
She chuckled as she walked into her cabin.

I wondered how she knew I was deathly afraid of bears. It was
almost dark and that washroom was not very close to the cabin. I
ran all the way, hoping the bears were all asleep for the winter. The
washroom turned out to be one of those unglamorous camp- style out
houses. It made me wonder more about this lovely lady and what kind
of beginnings she had so that coming to such a primitive place helped
her to feel grounded.

After a light dinner we settled down in front of the fireplace. She
handed me a cup of tea before curling up on the furry rug in front of
the fire. "My story begins with my Grandmother Olena, who lived in
The Ukraine during a time of political unrest and war."

Then she looked at me as if to make something clear and said,
"Ordinary people like you and me are caught in the suffering and
loss that war and political upheaval brings. When the last gun has
been put down and peace treaties signed, the war has still not ended.
People who have lost homes, land, property and culture are caught
up in the aftermath, sometimes for generations. Displaced people become minorities that are often unwanted and unwelcome. Their children suffer most because the parents are no longer the guiding light
they should be to the children. Keep this in mind and don't judge my
parents for what they did."

CHAPTER I

As a younger man, Ivan Burak had been outspoken against the
Soviet involvement in his homeland, Ukraine. To the surprise
of many he joined the Soviet Army for a time. After leaving the Army
he switched his allegiance to join the radical group "The National
Democratic Party". He was involved in many demonstrations and he
was vocal, too vocal. When the Galician Governor was assassinated
by a close friend of Ivan's, he was also considered a suspect since he
had spearheaded a revolt not long before. His name was never completely cleared.

Once Ivan completed University, he suddenly became politically
'silent'. However, he was not forgotten among the political circles who
lumped him in with right wing extremists. Because his withdrawal
from the political scene had been so abrupt, suspicions grew that he
had become a double agent.

Ivan gave little thought to his youthful activities as he settled into
married life with Olena, a young teacher from Kiev, who he had met
while they both attended University. They made their home in Kiev
where he established his dental practice. They soon had a daughter,
Nataliya and several years later, baby Anicha completed the little
family. Ivan did not realize for several years that his earlier political
involvement and his sudden life change made him a 'marked' man, as
different political factions struggled to control his country.

There was always political unrest in the Ukraine, but during the
summer of 1913 it intensified. To Ivan's surprise he was called in and
questioned by each and every political faction in the country that
summer.

He was not greatly concerned until he realized he was being
watched. He was heavily interrogated after he left Kiev for a week to
visit his ailing Mother. The interrogator knew exactly where he had

been and every person, he had spoken to during his time away from the city. He was accused of using his mother's illness as a cover for covert political involvement. Several times he was sure he was being followed as he went to work. It began to worry him a great deal.

Olena shared his concerns. Since two of her brothers were leaving for Canada, they decided it would be wise to join them and leave the Ukraine before the situation became worse. Plans were quickly made. Although it would be comparatively easy to travel by boat from Kiev to the port of Odessa, Ivan was uneasy. It would be too public. The recent interrogations made him feel uneasy and he felt they needed to leave as secretly as possible. Plans were made to leave Kiev in the darkest part of the night. They would go empty handed, with only the children. If anyone saw them leave the house it would not arouse any suspicion of them leaving the country.

Ivan's plan was to be at a certain point on a certain country road at daybreak. A man with a wagon load of hay was to meet them and hide them in his load. In this way they would travel to the little village in the Carpathians where Olena's brothers lived. From there they would travel to Odessa with the other families, dressed as peasants. They made their plans quietly, telling none of their friends.

The time set for departure came. Ivan went to work as usual. His secretary booked appointments for the future. Olena did laundry and hung it on the line. When it was dry, she took it in and hung more out which she did not bring in. Life went on as it usually did at their house on Mondays.

Ivan came home that evening, bringing a friend for the evening meal as he often did. The family sat around the table, enjoying the food and conversation. The girls, seven-year-old Nataliya and eighteen-month-old Anicha were put to bed at their usual bedtime. There was nothing anywhere to arouse suspicion. The friend left at ten and they put their lights out shortly after. If anyone was watching it would look like they had gone to bed at the time they always did.

At midnight they planned to wake their sleeping girls, then quietly slip out the door and walk away from the city. Ivan had often been down the country road they were to take so he knew exactly where to go and where all the shortcuts were.

Suddenly there was a heavy knock, followed by a splintering crash as two soldiers broke down the door and switched on the light.

They asked Ivan his name, then seized him at gunpoint, rushing him out without a chance to say "Goodbye" to Olena. But as he was being shoved out the door, he was able to turn his head just enough to mouth the word, "Go."

Olena stood in shock. Moments before they had held such hope of being free of wars and oppression. In that one moment, their dream was shattered, perhaps forever. The unknown future stretched out like a dark highway in a nightmare. Fear for Ivan. Fear for all of them crippled her mind. Ivan had told her to go. Perhaps he knew something she didn't. Were they all in danger?

As if in a dream she gently woke Nataliya and helped her into her jacket. She scooped Anicha into the shawl along with the bag of dry bread and a flask of water. Tying the shawl around her, she took Nataliya's hand and they stepped out in the darkness, frightened, alone and unsure where they were going.

She walked through the city, glad that they lived near the edge. Even then, it was a long walk. She wished that Ivan would have told her the name of the street that connected to the country road. She had no idea where she was going or where that road was. She eventually found a country road that she hoped was the right one. They walked for what seemed like miles down that dusty road. Daylight came. They watched eagerly for the wagon with its load of hay. No wagon came. They walked on. The girls were hungry, so she soaked some bread in a little water, fed them and ate a little herself, before she nursed Anicha. After that little rest they just kept walking and walking. There was no load of hay and she felt panic rising in her throat-- like a noose. She had no idea what to do now or where to go. She was exhausted. Nataliya had blisters on both her heels and was crying with every step. If that wagon would come, they could lie down on the soft hay and rest. But the wagon never came. As darkness came, she had no choice but to pull her exhausted girls close to her and try to sleep on the cold ground beside the narrow road. She woke in the night. Panic choked her again as thoughts raced through her mind. What had gone wrong?" Had she taken the wrong road?" Ivan had known the connecting street number, but he had never told her, thinking they would be walking together. What should she do now? Should she go back? If she went back where would they go next? She felt lost and unsure of herself. Two little lives depended on her.

Morning came. A grey drizzly, cold morning. Olena felt miserable and Nataliya's blistered heels were bleeding. The mother tore strips from her undergarment to make bandages for her child's feet. It helped a little. She soaked more bread. They ate. They cried as she made the decision to keep walking. If it was the right road, and they could get there riding in a load of hay, she should be able to eventually walk there. It would just take longer.

Several times peasants with wagons loaded with wheat or cabbage came by and invited them to ride along. Realizing that it was probably not herself or the children that needed to be hidden, she gladly accepted each and every ride that was offered. She asked each one how far it was to the village where her brothers lived but none of them had heard of the village. Thankfully, one farmer refilled the water flask, and another gave them a little bag of apples.

Nataliya's feet were so painful now that she sobbed with every step. Olena was exhausted from carrying the heavy toddler. Thankfully another wagon came, and they rode until the farmer left the road to go to his field. It was still daylight, but they could not walk any further. She led Nataliya to a spot behind a clump of trees near the road, hoping to find some shelter from the pouring rain. They were cold and miserable, and the trees gave little protection. They ate more bread and munched apples. As soon as they finished their simple meal, Olena soaked the blood caked bandages and removed them from the child's feet. By the time this was done Anicha was shivering. The mother and sister curled around the little one try to keep her warm. Their coats and the shawl were soaked and the only warmth they had was where their bodies touched.

Another grey drizzly morning followed. They woke chilled, wet and miserable. There was only a little bread left and Olena gave it to the children. Nataliya's feet were bandaged with new strips of cloth and the weary group began another day of walking. Early that day another wagon stopped, and the driver asked them where they were going. "Hop on then", he said, when she named the village. "You are going in the wrong direction to reach that village, but I can take you to the trail that connects to the right road. I am going that way anyway, so I would be happy to take you".

There was room in the wagon for the girls to lie down. Anicha kicked her legs joyfully, glad to be free from the confines of the soggy shawl. Olena sat beside them, wishing there was a place to rest her own chilled, aching body better, yet so thankful not to have to walk and carry the baby. Her arms felt like they were on fire and her back hurt even worse. She hoped the journey was almost over and they would be closer to the village.

At noon the man stopped to rest and feed his horses before pulling out a box of food. He smiled. "I was taking this to my old Mother, but she is going to understand when I tell her I gave it to a poor woman and her children."

He opened a jug of soup, poured some in a cup and handed it to Nataliya along with a chunk of black bread and a piece of cheese. Next, he filled the cup for Olena, handing her an even larger chunk of bread and cheese. For Anicha, he tore up little pieces of bread and soaked it in broth from the soup. Olena fed her with her fingers. The little child gulped the food hungrily. When they finished the soup, he brought out a pan of cabbage rolls and shared them as well. Nothing had ever tasted so good to the hungry, exhausted group.

The children slept again as the wagon jolted and bumped its way down the road. Olena, uncomfortable as she was, dozed off for a little while. When she woke, she saw that the terrain had changed and there were more hills and trees. Her brothers lived somewhere in the Carpathians. For the first time she felt hope that she might still get to her brother's home in time to board the ship.

The shadows were getting long when the man brought his horses to a stop. The road turned sharply to the right while a faint, narrow trail led to the left. "This trail will lead you to the road you should have taken," he said. "It is still a good three day walk down this trail though, until you come to the road you should have been on. That road is well travelled, and you should be able to get rides all the way to the village where you want to go," he added as he filled their water flask. He paused and looked at them for a moment then gave them his flask of milk, a loaf of bread and a bit of cheese before driving away. Olena could hardly find the words to thank him, but just stood there crying as he waved and went on his way.

They had only walked a short distance down the trail that evening before they had to stop. Nataliya's feet were giving her unbearable pain. Thankful to find a place for the night that had trees for shelter, and moss to cushion them Olena thankfully put Anicha on the ground. Nataliya sank into the soft moss and tried to pull her shoes off. She couldn't. They were stuck to the bandages and the bandages were stuck to her heels. It took a lot of soaking and painful effort to finally get her feet out of the shoes. Once the bandages were off, Olena realized in horror that the blisters were no longer just raw and bleeding. They were infected and oozing. After cleansing them as best she could with a little water, she did not rebandage them, hoping the air would dry them.

Nataliya's feet were no better by morning. She tried to put her shoes on her swollen feet. It was impossible. In desperation Olena took Anicha's little quilted jacket and tied it around one of the girl's feet with strips torn from her own dress. Then she bound Nataliya's own jacket around the other foot. She draped her own coat around the older girl's shoulders and hoped the heat from her own body would be enough to keep the shawl-wrapped toddler warm.

The walk was agonizing. The baby seemed even heavier and the pain in Olena's back was intense. Nataliya cried out with every step. Realizing that they could not go any farther that day, the mother soon found another soft sheltered spot to rest. They ate the last of the food. She hoped if they had a day of resting Nataliya's feet would heal enough to walk the following day. It was not to be. If anything, they were worse by morning.

They could hear the gurgling of a stream somewhere off the trail. In extreme pain, Nataliya dragged herself behind her mother until they found the stream. Olena settled her suffering child on the stream bank where the clear gurgling water could cleanse and sooth the pain in her little feet. They rested by the stream all day. A few berries grew there. It was not enough to stop the pangs of hunger but enough to give them a little strength for the long journey ahead of them.

There would be no journey the next day. Nataliya cried most of the night. By morning she was flushed and fiery with fever; her feet red and swollen even more. Walking was out of the question. They spent the day much the same as the day before, with Nataliya's feet in the stream. Olena scouted around for more berries and mushrooms but found little. Anicha cried incessantly. By evening the baby was coughing and she was also burning with fever. The little girls lay side by side on the ground. Helplessly, the mother curled around both her children, covering them with the shawl. She had not thought of the possibility of them dying before. Now the specter of death hovered over her like a cold, black blanket of fear. Should she leave her little ones and try to find help? But no! She had heard animals howling in the night. She did not know what a wolf howl was like, but she knew something was out there. She would stay with her children until the end.

CHAPTER 2

Olena never remembered how long they were there. Was it only a day or was it two or three? The hours and days and nights blended together in a blur of hunger, worry and grief. From time to time she dribbled water in the girl's mouths, thankful for the little stream and the fact they at least had water. Then she would curl around them again to keep them warm and doze off, knowing that they would probably die there, together.

It was a middle-aged woman who found them. She was searching for medicinal herbs along the banks of the stream when she saw what she thought were three bodies almost hidden in the bushes. Her first thought was to hurry back to her village and get help, but being a curious woman, decided she would check them out first. She approached cautiously and thought maybe she detected the motion of breathing. Cautiously she reached out her hand to touch Olena who woke with a start and a scream. The poor lady sank to the ground in her fright, but within moments collected her wits once more.

She could see the situation was critical. Without questions, she pulled Nataliya over her strong shoulders and motioned for Olena to carry Anicha. The toddler hung limply as Olena lifted her. The weight of the child was almost more than she could carry. She staggered behind as the woman led them back the short distance to the trail where she had a horse and cart tied. "I will take you to my home," the lady said, as she untied the horse.

Weak, and unsure if she was awake or dreaming, Olena pushed the girls onto the cart and struggled up beside them. The girls did not cry but moaned each time the cart wheel hit a rut in the road. She hoped help had not come too late for her little ones.

The ride to the woman's village was long and the road was rough. Pain is bearable when there is hope and Olena felt hope as she tried to cushion her little ones with her own body. At last the woman pulled the horse to a stop beside a small house and helped the travelers down from the cart. Olena slumped to the ground, unable to walk on her own strength. The lady tenderly carried the children inside and lay them on quilts by the fire before returning to help Olena to her feet.

Within minutes the women of the village gathered around to help. Soon the girls were having warm broth spooned down their throats. The woman who had rescued them prepared a pail with hot water, salt and herbs to soak Nataliya's feet, then wrapped them in a poultice made of old bread, milk and herbs. Olena was given a heaping bowl of soup and some black bread. She took the bowl with trembling hands but was unable to get the spoon to her mouth. Seeing this, a kind Baba sat beside her and slowly fed her.

One of the ladies volunteered to stay to care for the girls all night. She wrapped them in warm quilts and alternated spoons of broth with nasty tasting medicine until their fevers broke. At last the little ones sank into a deep restful sleep. Olena lay beside them, thankful for the miracle that they were even found; thankful for the kindness of these strangers who had saved their lives. Still, her troubled mind ran in circles, wondering what to do next. The girls were too sick to travel. She had asked the lady who had cared for the children through the night what the date was. The ship would leave in three more days so there was no possibility of going to Canada. She could not return to Kiev and the unrest in the city. She worried over Ivan. What had happened to him? Maybe, just maybe, she thought, "they only questioned him and let him go. He would have taken the right road and would leave on that ship". That thought gave her a measure of peace and dried her endless tears. Sleep finally came.

The villagers had many questions for Olena the following day. They listened as she told them of their plan to go to Canada, of her husband being forced into what she feared was the Soviet Army, her hope that he had been released and would be able to get away to a new country and away from oppression.

She told them the story of her long and painful journey. Of taking the wrong road and going in the wrong direction. Now she had no place for her and her children to go. Her brothers were leaving for Canada in a couple of days and she would have no family there after the brothers left. She could not return to Kiev, even if were safe for her to do so, as she could not afford to live there without Ivan's income. She had not taught for several years and to try to get a position now would be impossible.

The villagers listened, then quietly left. That evening several of the ladies returned and asked her if she would be willing to live in their village and teach their children. They could not afford to pay her wages but would supply them with a house and food. Also, many of the younger men had joined the army and they could use more help with the farm work. Feeling she had no other choice, she agreed. Her journey had ended. This would be her home.

CHAPTER 3

I t took time for the two girls to get well. Little Anicha's cough lasted for weeks. Olena worried and wished there was a doctor to take her to, but that was impossible. She had to rely on the special care and herbal medicine the woman gave her little girl. It was new to her, but as she watched her little one slowly regaining her strength she was thankful for the folk wisdom that helped her child. Nataliya responded much sooner. Within a couple of days, the bread poultices had cleared the infection. Her feet healed quickly after that and within days she was out and about, exploring the village and getting to know everyone.

They were soon settled in their new home, a humble structure with a clay stove for heat and an attached shed for cows. The moment Nataliya learned what the shed was for she began begging for a cow. For her mother, having a cow was unthinkable. Cows smell bad, they were noisy, and she did not want one. "Better to get milk from the Healer than we keep a cow," she would say each time the subject of a cow came up. "I am a teacher of children, not a peasant woman to milk cows."

It was a beautiful autumn afternoon when Nataliya came skipping home, smiling as only she could smile, carrying a wooden stool and a pail. Beside her was an elderly man, leading a cow. As soon as he had the cow tied in the shed, he gave a 'how to milk a cow lesson' to the little girl. She seemed to be a natural for the job. She was soon milking the cow as if this was something she had done every day of her life. With a little bow the man said, "Every family needs their own cow," and left, leaving Olena wondering how to survive sharing her home with a cow. There seemed no way to get rid of the beast without breaking her daughter's heart and offending the old man as well. The cow stayed and was Nataliya's special task from then on.

Village life was very different than city life. Olena had many challenges with the changes. With the help of the peasant women she learned to grow a garden and preserve food for "the hungry times." One of her big adjustments at first was learning to use the big clay oven that took up a great deal of space in her home. Eventually she was making passable bread, but young Nataliya, ever the adventurous one, took over the job of family baker as soon as she was strong enough.

In spite of the challenges in adjusting to peasant life, Olena loved teaching the children. Even without the books and helps she was used to, the children in the little school learned well under her tutelage. The people in the village made her feel welcome and she soon felt she belonged and was needed.

Anicha was a gentle child. She reminded her mother of a quiet stream. Always predictable, always calm. As she grew older, she was much loved by all the Babas in the village. She would help the old ones in any way she could, from washing dishes to digging and cleaning vegetables. She was a plain child, yet her sweetness made her beautiful to all.

Nataliya was a complete opposite. She had looks that took her a step above beautiful. She was also daring and fearless, a fact which got her into no end of trouble when she was younger. No matter what she was dared to do, she would do it. Other mother's in the village ordered their children never to dare her to climb on, jump off of, or swim anything. They did not want to feel responsible if the Burak girl met an untimely end during one of her escapades. It seemed that she was being rescued from one death defying adventure to another, and Olena always felt thankful when night came, and her multi-bruised child was safely asleep.

As she grew older, Nataliya eagerly learned all she could about farming and volunteered to help with every farm task. Still daring, she had no fear of any of the farm animals. The woman who had found them in the forest was known in the peasant village as the 'Healer.' She and the girl soon formed a special bond. When the woman gathered herbs, Nataliya was at her heels, learning the names of the herbs and how they were used. When there were sick animals to treat, the girl was with her. The Healer would not let her go with her when she treated sick people for fear the girl would fall ill, yet she always described the illness and what herbs were best to help give the person a nudge back to health.

There was more to Nataliya than fearless daring and a thirst for knowledge. She was always singing and dancing, a fact that brought endless sunshine to the residents of the village. There were so many political troubles during those days and to see one so beautiful, so happy, so full of hope and music helped them forget the troubles around them for a little while. Whenever a villager was outside and heard her beautiful voice in song, they would stop whatever they were doing to listen. Some were sure she was a beautiful angel sent directly from Heaven to bring joy to the village.

Her mother did not always share the opinion that Nataliya was an angel! Yes, she was always happily singing and dancing, she had an unending thirst to learn, but the girl had another side to her. She was headstrong. If she wanted to do something, she did it. Dire warnings that danger, disaster and even death could result from her decisions did nothing to deter her.

She was so like her father, Olena thought. "Ivan the Fearless," his friends used to call him. Olena used to call him that too, as she combed her fingers through his dark, curly hair. Her fearless Ivan was gone now, but Nataliya was his little replica in so many ways. With all the love in her mother heart, she worried over her child and feared for her future. That fearless nature had taken her husband from her and she worried endlessly over her daughter and what would become of her.

CHAPTER 4

The years went on. There were many smaller uprisings in Kiev before the 1917 failed attempt at Ukrainian Independence. The following year was "The Big War as they called World War One" Olena prayed and hoped that Ivan was not part of any of this. The people of Ukraine wanted freedom, but freedom seemed out of reach while different factions fought to rule the country. She worried about what future her two children would face as they grew up.

Life that had always been hard in the peasant villages became even harder. Many of the young men had gone to war and would never be coming back. There was grief. It was best to keep working hard and not think about a future beyond the day they were living in. Olena wondered how life was for her brothers in Canada. Had they found the peace they were hoping for? There were many rumors that the immigrants from the Ukraine had been jailed there because of the war, since the Canadian Government did not trust their loyalty. She hoped these were only stories and that some place in this earth there could be peace.

Everyone in the village was immediately suspicious when a tall, dark and extremely handsome stranger came to the village asking for refuge. He claimed to be a relative of the murdered Romanov family and was in fear for his own life. He said his name was Peter Romanov and begged for refuge. The village buzzed with curiosity and not a little concern. Most believed he was a spy, sent by the Soviets to see how much food they grew. This man was obviously from Russia, but only a few believed he was the person he said he was.

There was great speculation that instead of being connected to the deceased royal family he was instead a Ruska Roma, a Russian Gypsy. They knew that a few years before this, the Soviets had destroyed an entire Gypsy village in Russia. Many gypsies had fled to other countries. Maybe this Peter was from that village and had been wandering since then. Some thought that perhaps he was both Gypsy and related to the Romanovs since there were always scandals among the rich. They soon learned that whoever he was, he was a talented musician. His hands looked as if he had never worked in his life. This made the villagers with their calloused hands, even more wary about him living there.

Only one person offered him a place to stay. It was a very old man who did not seem to care that this stranger might be a liar, a spy, a gypsy or a member of Russian Royalty. "He is human" the old man said. "If he wants to hurt us, he will do it whether he has a place to stay or not. I will be kind to him because his music feeds my old, sad heart."

Peter stayed on. Soon most of the villagers were won over by his charming smile and his great gift of music. On warm evenings he would go out to the little village square and play his violin. A crowd of peasants, tired from their day of heavy farm work, would soon gather to be refreshed by his music. In that crowd was a tall, beautiful teenage girl who always sang as he played his violin. She did not know the songs but put words, beautiful words to the music he played. One evening he asked her to join him in the square. They sang together, and the beauty of their blended voices left all the villagers in awe. Everyone, that is, except Olena. Her mother wisdom sensed trouble ahead and she was furious. "There have never been two more beautiful people with such beautiful voices in our village before," some said. "Theirs are the voices of angels," said others. To Olena, if he was indeed an angel, then he was an angel from a dark place. She wanted him to stay away from her daughter and go back to wherever he came from.

As soon as she could entice Nataliya to leave the square that evening, she rushed her home. "You are only a fifteen-year-old child. You don't know this man. None of us do. He is older than you and who knows where he has been or what he is up to now. This man can destroy you and your whole future," she warned. "You are not to ever sing with him again. If fact you are not to ever see him again."

Nataliya had never listened to her mother before and she wouldn't now. She and Peter continued to sing together. She would dance and sing as he played the violin in the evenings. Soon they began walking together, through the village and into the surrounding fields, singing as they went. The peasants would listen from where ever they were working. To them it seemed like the sun shone brighter and the crops looked better when they heard the songs. Poor Olena warned and wept, but Nataliya only laughed at her mother's warnings and spent most of every day with Peter.

News about the talented singers spread from village to village and it was not long until they were invited to another village. When the request came for her and Peter to sing in that village, the girl went without telling her mother. When Olena found out she was gone, her concern for her daughter's safety knew no bounds. She wanted to get hold of that no-good Peter and send him running.

Nataliya came home two days later. She found her mother out furiously chopping wood for the fire. "Peter and I are going to get married and travel around doing concerts together," she blurted out.

Olena crashed her axe into the chopping block and turned to her daughter, her face scarlet with anger. She had enough of her daughter's foolishness and it would end now! "You will do no such a thing! " She shouted. "There is no way I am going to let you marry that Russian or Gypsy, whichever he is. I don't want you to ever see him again! I won't let you see him again. I won't even let you leave this house and he must leave this village and go back to wherever he came from."

She stood in front of her daughter giving her the look that only a very angry Mother is capable of giving to a headstrong child who is putting himself or herself in danger. The girl only smiled at her mother and said nothing. That evening she sneaked out of the house and joined Peter in the square. When the singing was over, she and Peter walked hand in hand to her mother's house. She would not let them in.

Hours later, Nataliya sneaked in quietly. Her mother was waiting up for her. "Mother," she spoke softly so as not to wake Anicha. "Peter and I have been asked to perform together in many cities. I want to marry him first but if you won't allow that, I am going to go with him anyway. We will leave tomorrow unless you let us marry first."

With her heart breaking, the mother finally consented to the marriage. At least her wayward girl would not leave in disgrace if they left as man and wife. Peter and Nataliya immediately announced their plan to marry. There was a great deal of excitement in the little village as all the women gathered to help plan the wedding. Olena envied the excitement and happiness of the village women, but she felt none of it. Her only emotion was fear for her daughter and a fury that wound around every thought she had of Peter. She hated him. Cloaked in her anger, she did little in preparing for the event. Someone else found a white dress that fit the girl as if it had been made for her. Another found a veil. A wonderful wedding meal was made from the little the villagers had.

The day of the wedding was on the day of the leaving. Olena slowly walked her daughter to the little church while tears streamed down her face. Suddenly Nataliya stopped and pulled her mother close. "Mother," she said, "I know you don't like Peter and you are worried about me and very sad. But the love I have for Peter is like the love you have for my father. No matter where we go and what happens in our lives, I will always love him. I will always love you too, Mother. Now, please tell me you love me and are happy for me. I will need your blessing to follow me through life". Olena hugged her beautiful child close, but she could find no words to say except a tearful, "I love you".

The couple left the village as soon as the meal was over. Olena and Anicha walked slowly back to the little house that now seemed silent and dark without Nataliya in it. They sat and cried until suddenly Anicha snuffled back some tears and asked, "Which of us has to milk that smelly cow tonight?" They laughed together, glad for something to ground them again. Between the two of them they eventually managed to milk the unhappy beast. They agreed that it would be wise to give the cow to someone else and hope that person would give them a little milk in return. Nataliya had made her own choices. Now they would make theirs and they agreed. The cow must go, and it must go before morning or they would have to milk her again! In the deepening dusk they led the cow to the home of a young couple who were overjoyed to have another cow and promised them fresh milk every day.

CHAPTER 5

Three years went by. They had heard nothing from Nataliya. Her mother lay awake many nights wondering what had happened to her daughter. It was as if she had vanished from the earth the day she married Peter. She had sweet, sensible, dependable Anicha, the kind of daughter to bring joy to any mother's heart. Yet she missed her wild child with every fiber of her being, and in missing her she struggled with a deepening hatred toward Peter. If he hadn't come to their village, her Nataliya would be home and safe. Where was she now? Maybe in Russia somewhere living with a band of Ruska Roma? Maybe it was worse, and she was not living anymore. A mother with a missing child knows no peace of mind or rest until she knows where her loved one is. Olena kept her concerns to herself, but the worry was un-ending.

The knock came early one September morning. Anicha, still half asleep, answered the door. There stood Nataliya, with a suitcase in her hand. The younger girl screamed out her sister's name with such joy that Olena came on the run. Swooping her daughter in her arms, she led her in and sat her on a chair by the fire.

After a cup of hot milk and a piece of black bread, she explained to her mother that Peter had found a job on a ship going to Canada. Once he was there, he was going to find work. He would send for her as soon as he had a place to live and enough money for her passage on the ship. In the meantime, he had sent her back to be with her mother. "As you can see, Mother, I am pregnant," she said. "I want to be with you when I have the baby and have a place for the baby and I to stay until Peter sends for me."

Olena couldn't speak. She was overjoyed to see her daughter again, yes, but not abandoned like this. Her fury towards Peter now was beyond description. How dare he do this to her daughter. He took her away and now that she was pregnant, he had abandoned her and ran off to another country. This was her daughter that he had used and abandoned. She wondered if it was wrong to hope he would be shipwrecked on the way to Canada and they would have him out of their lives forever.

She wanted to tell Nataliya that he would never come back but seeing the hope in the young woman's face she bit back the words. The poor girl would find out soon enough. In the meantime, she would not crush the glow of hope in her daughter's eyes. She finally managed to say, "I am glad you are home," but the hatred she felt for Peter was like a fire that would burn for a very long time.

Nataliya was soon right at home again, laughing, singing and bubbling over with plans for her new life in Canada when Peter would send her the money to join him. Her baby was due in January and she was excited about this new life too. Secretly, Olena feared the girl would never settle down long enough to have a baby, let alone take care of it.

Settle down she did when the pains brought her to her knees. "I can't do this", she cried, clutching her mother's hand in a crushing grip. Many hours later, with the encouragement of her mother and the experienced help of the midwife, little Katja finally entered the world of waiting adults. Nataliya lay back, exhausted; the battle for her child's life hard fought but won.

Olena held the tiny child to her heart, surprised at the feeling of love that rushed through her. Yes, she was Peter's child and Nataliya's child, but she was also part of herself; part of Ivan. She would carry the strengths of the Grandparents, but she would go far beyond their lives. She was the future. She prayed for a life of peace for this little one. She lay the baby on Nataliya's chest as she stroked her own daughter's hair and kissed the forehead wet with perspiration. It was a day for rejoicing.

A few days later, Nataliya received a letter from Peter. He had reached Canada and had found work on the railway. Happy to have an address at last, she soon sent him a letter letting him know that their little daughter had been born. Olena felt her fury against Peter calm a tiny fraction. At least he had written to his wife. Maybe there was some degree of good in the man after all, although she seriously doubted it.

Little Katjia was a healthy, happy baby. Black curls framed her soft tan face. The brown eyes that looked like they belonged to a baby fawn, took in everything there was to see. Rosy cheeks and a wonderful little mouth that almost always smiled. This was Katja. Her complexion was darker than her father's. The villagers looked at her and nodded their heads in agreement about who Peter was and nicknamed her the "Little Gypsy". They all agreed that she was the most beautiful child they had ever seen and whatever her ancestry was, it created beauty.

She was far too little to understand the increasing hardships around her. Ever changing Government rule was tightening a noose around the villagers. They were forced to sell almost everything they grew, leaving a shortage of food. There would have been immediate starvation except for cleverly hidden gardens and little grain stashes. Nataliya got another cow and the family had milk again. This time she managed to inspire her sister to learn to milk the cow so that when she left this time, they would have an extra source of food.

Time went by and there was no more word from Peter, which did not surprise Olena. She had already decided he was a worthless scoundrel who had left his wife and child. Deep in the most selfish corner of her heart she was glad he hadn't written. She dreaded the thought of Nataliya and precious Little Katjia leaving her. Still when she looked in the lonely eyes of her daughter, she hoped he would make good on his promise. She knew the feeling of having the man she loved torn from her side and missing. She could not wish this kind of pain on her own child. More than that, she did want her daughter somewhere safe and far away from the constant unrest and worry of the homeland. She struggled to find peace with the mix of emotions that battled in her mind.

Eventually, Olena began to hold a hope close to her heart that perhaps Peter would be the means of them all escaping the oppression that surrounded them. It was only a tiny hope but event the smallest hope can bring peace in troubled times. Yet as the time passed with no word from Peter, she was also trying to find somewhere that she could provide a better life for her family. Anicha wanted to leave the village. She dreamed of being a doctor and wanted an opportunity to have an education. There was no future in the village for the girl and Olena understood her restlessness.

CHAPTER 6

Whatever dreams of instant wealth Peter may have had, they were quickly dashed when he left the ship and stepped on Canadian soil. There were no open arms and job offers for anyone from Russia. It was only by chance that he found a job on the railway during his first month in the new country. Some railway worker had been killed on the job. Just by chance Peter had showed up asking for a job before anyone knew there had been a tragedy.

His happiness in having a job was short. He had grown up in a wealthy family and had never done menial work before. By the end of the first day of swinging the great hammer, his soft hands were blistered and bleeding. His arms and back hurt so badly he could not sleep on the hard bunk he had been provided with. Only desperation held him to the job. Eventually he could do the heavy work without serious pain, although his hands stiffened and often ached in the night. He spent the first year working on the railroad. As his work on the railroad reached the Prairies, he left the railroad job and began helping with grain harvests in the fall. For more than the next three years, he alternated between helping with harvests, working as a farm hand on a dairy farm and a stint at logging during the winter which he found as painful as working on the railroad.

He knew Nataliya was a farmer at heart and he realized he liked that way of life the best of what he had tried. In his travels as a harvest worker he saw many farms that were poor, but there was one communitythat he decided would be a perfect place to settle in and call home. Every farm in that community looked prosperous. He had been in the area several times, helping with harvests, haying and general farm work. Each time he worked there, his decision to purchase land and start a dairy farm grew firmer. He knew basically nothing about dairy farming, but most of the farms in this community were dairy farms. These farmers appeared to be doing well, with comfortable homes and well cared for premises. This would be the life he would want for his own family. Dairy farming could not be that hard and Nataliya did seem to like her cow so he felt sure she would gladly accept this decision.

He had made a friend in the community by the name of Jack, who was not a farmer himself, but he did seem quite involved in farming. Friend Jack seemed willing to answer the young man's many questions regarding dairy farming. It was good to have a friend like this; so willing to help him when he still had a hard time with English and knew little about farming.

Peter had been saving all the money he could, hoping to have enough to find a place to live and bring his little family to join him. Now that he knew where he wanted to live, he turned to his friend Jack for advice on how to buy land in this community. With a big grin, Jack told him there was a Mr. Ardythe who was the only one that could sell him land him in that community.

Bill Ardythe had inherited billions. While still a young man he left Britain and came to Canada with the plan of purchasing three adjacent townships of excellent land. He managed to get it quite cheaply. In turn he would sell land to prospective farmers and personally provide them with financing for land, buildings, machinery and livestock; whatever was needed to get the farm up and showing a profit in as short a time as possible. It worked well for most as he did not pressure them as long as they managed to pay the interest on the loan every year. If they ended up unable to pay, he was not concerned. He would have his land back along with the interest they paid and the improvements they had made. He could sell it for more next time around if the buildings were up and the farm functional. It worked well for him and also for most of the purchasers. He was reasonable and never pressured his clients as long as they were making an effort to make payments. He was merciless, though, if anyone could not meet the payments. Illness or a death usually caused some financial hardship, but Mr. Ardythe cut no one any slack. "Can't pay. Can't stay," was one of his mottos.

Foreclosures were rare though and most of his purchasers appeared to be doing well. Very few farms had telephone service or electricity during that era, but he laid out some extra millions to have his farm community enjoy the same luxuries the folks in towns had. In reality, very few of the farmers made enough to pay much on equity, but they lived in comfort. Paying the interest only, which was all most could do, could be considered paying rent. Some never tried to pay on the equity, preferring to salt away any extra toward retirement. It seemed to work for most and it was a way for farmers to get started and make a decent living.

The old man's racial discriminations were strong. He termed anyone from Slavic Countries as 'Bohunks.' Natives he called 'Injuns' and colored folk were classed as 'Niggers.' He bragged to his cronies that this community would never have any Injuns, Niggers or Bohunks living in it because he would not sell them land. The very ones that had lost everything and needed that helping hand to have a home and a means of income would never get that help from him.

Peter knew none of this as he went into Mr. Ardythe's office. What Jack had told him sounded like a dream come true. Mr. Ardythe would sell him land and provide financing for the land, farm buildings, cattle and everything he would need to get started in his dairy business. It would be perfect. With the money he had saved he could bring Nataliya over and they could begin the beautiful life they dreamed of. He would have enough to send for Olena and Anicha as well. Their good life was about to begin! He was whistling merrily as he headed for Mr Ardyth's office.

His dream was dashed in moments. He never understood the exact words Mr. Ardythe used as he ordered him out of his office. He just knew that there was no chance of getting land this way since he and all his kind were the scum of the earth and he was not welcome in this community.

Jack was full of sympathy when Peter told him that Mr. Ardythe would not sell him land. He then gave Peter some hope that he might still obtain property in the area. It would not be quite as easy to get started without the extra financing, but a family could still make a good living by finding some land they could homestead. It would only cost him ten dollars and he would have to guarantee he would build a home and cultivate forty acres within the next three years.

Peter was delighted when Jack told him there was some nearby land available to homestead. Although it was in a different township, it adjoined Mr. Ardythe's home place. In fact, they would be close neighbors. Peter was not sure being a close neighbor to Mr Ardyth was what he wanted after being yelled at and insulted by this man, yet being able to get land near this prosperous community seemed like a good thing. Especially since Jack would be there to give him a helping hand and advice.

Jack went with Peter to see the land and pointed out acres of what appeared to be grassy meadows. "You will have no end of hay and pasture here. Won't even have to clear any land before you cultivate unless you want to. You have some wooded land to build your house on and some more areas of higher land farther on but most of it is this beautiful open meadow just like you see here. This is one pretty place wouldn't you say, my friend?" Jack clapped his hand on Peter's shoulder as he spoke. "By the way, I will set you up with 6 cows and some hay in the spring after you get your barn built and a few fences up. Pay me now and I will have them for you as soon as you are ready. You can start out by selling cream until you get established in the dairy business. It's pretty good money and will give you a good way to start." Jack smiled his friendly smile as he named a price per cow. Peter willingly agreed. It was good to have a friend like Jack. Speaking English was still a struggle for him so having Jack take care of buying the cattle would put his mind at ease.

To Peter, that land was a beautiful sight. It was autumn. The gold and red of the deciduous trees on the hills contrasted with evergreens, while many acres of tall, golden grass rippled in the wind. He had found his place in this new land so filled with opportunity. Excitement filled him as he looked across that beautiful meadow and thought how Nataliya would love it.

Within a few days he had the paperwork done. He would build a dugout home and a pole barn. Of course, it would be temporary. They would soon be able to build a nice house and a big barn like other farmers had.

There was not much money left after paying Jack for the cows and sending off the money to Nataliya for her trip to Canada, but if he were careful, he would have enough for food until next summer. By then they would have income from selling cream.

Jack generously gave him a few sacks each of cull carrots and potatoes. "One guy saved this for his hog feed," he grinned. "But there are lots good spuds in there. Too good for the hogs anyway so I convinced him the Big Rus would need some food. Can't see my friend go hungry while the hogs are eaten' them good spuds. You need to sort them pretty quick though, and get them in a cold, dark place."

Peter accepted the vegetables with a grateful heart. Jack then lent him a spade, pick, axe and saw. "You are going to need them to make that dugout home," Jack grinned again. "Use em' until you get your building done and I'll pick them up next spring when I bring the cows."

Peter had recently worked for a farmer in another community. The man had not been able to pay wages but had given Peter a horse and an old wagon. It was a long walk to get them and he was glad he could ride home. Just having this animal of his own made him feel he was a part of this new land he owned. That night he wrote to tell Nataliya the wonderful news and all about the help his friend Jack was giving him and sent her the money for her passage on the ship

CHAPTER 7

It was December when the letter with the money came. Nataliya's scream of joy could be heard almost over the entire village. Peter had been gone for over two years and everyone pitied her, sure that he had abandoned her and the child. But no! He had sent money for her, and his letter said he had a farm and was building them a home.

There were hurdles to being able to leave Ukraine and more to get into Canada but finally both countries agreed to allow her and the child to be reunited with her husband. The wait was long, but the anticipation of being with Peter again kept her going through that long hungry winter. She wished her mother and sister could come too, but Peter had said he did not have enough money yet. In a couple of years maybe they could send for them, he was sure of that.

While she waited for time to pass, she tried to learn English. Olena had studied English in school so she wrote all the words she remembered and taught her daughter what they meant. It wasn't much but she could ask some basic questions. The Healer insisted she take a good supply of healing herbs and bags of garden seeds with her just in case she needed them and couldn't find them in the new country.

She worried a lot about leaving her mother behind. Olena did not seem well. Perhaps it was because she ate so little, making sure there was enough food for her own daughters and Little Katja. If that was the case it would be better after she left, as her mother would have more food. Anicha would have to milk the cow of course. No excuses this time as they would need the milk and cheese for food.

****

Peter eagerly drove his horse to his new farm. Excitement filled him. He would have to dig a hole in the sidehill for the home. His plan was to dig deep enough to get the pole front in place and then keep digging the cavern bigger during the winter. He would need to cut poles for the house, the barn and for firewood before winter.

His first task was to decide exactly where to make the home. He had not walked over much of the land with Jack. At the time Jack had pointed out where he should build it, but Peter wanted to see all his land before he started the huge job ahead of him. He spent the day happily wandering through brush and forest, over the open meadows for a short distance, then through more brush until he came to a growth of evergreens with a gem of a little lake nestled there. There was higher land overlooking the lake that had no underbrush or larger trees, only a heavy growth of very young poplars. It was as if the land had been cleared in that area at one time.

On the sidehill he found a depression with young poplars growing out of it. Looking closer he realized it had been a dugout home that had been filled in, but a few roof poles were still showing. He found a well nearby with a rusty bucket still attached to a pulley for drawing water. Someone had indeed been here before him. There was a large flat area covered with little poplars. It looked like it had been ploughed at some time. It worried him a little. Why had they left? They had certainly chosen a beautiful spot for a home. Why didn't they succeed? In spite of the niggling concerns, he decided to check the depression where the home had been. It would certainly be easier to pull the old poles out and shovel the soft dirt than it would be to dig a new dugout in the hard ground.

It was late by the time he finished checking out the area. He went back to where he had left his horse and wagon and drove them along the faint trail to the chosen home site. He would sleep in the wagon and get an early start in the morning.

Work on the home began at first light. Hitching his horse to the poles made removing them quite easy. It did not take long. To Peter's joy, once the poles were gone, he could see that there was not a great deal of dirt to be removed. After clambering over the pile of dirt he discovered the back part was in perfect condition, the roof poles still strong and undecayed. It was far larger than he imagined it would be. It must have been for a big family as pole boxes for several beds lined one wall. At the far end was a stove that had been made from a barrel. It stood upright so there was a small flat surface to cook on. There was a makeshift oven of sorts made of a smaller barrel fastened around the stovepipe. A large enamel pot stood on the stove, a pile of tin bowls, some spoons and a large, sharp knife lay on the dirt floor beside the stove. At the back was a door of poles. This led to another good-sized cavern which he realized was probably for storing vegetables. He felt like he had found a gold mine! Happily, he went to the wagon for the carrots and potatoes Jack had given him and after taking the time to sort the rotten ones out, he put them in the cool dark cavern. Here they would keep fresh and crisp for months to come. He tripped over something in the dark cavern while putting the vegetables away. Curious he brought it out to the light where he could see it. It was a strange looking can made of heavy metal, wide for much of the way to the top, then narrowing to a neck with a tight-fitting lid on it. It was a perfect place to keep the dry beans he had purchased.

He spent several days removing dirt from the entry of the dugout. The job was finally done, and new poles were cut to replace the broken ones. He was ready to begin rebuilding, and as the days grew colder and shorter, he knew he had to hurry. After a quick trip to town to purchase a hammer, nails, matches and a little food, he hurried back to the job. He knew nothing about farming, but he had a natural skill as a builder. Within a few days he had the front part of the home re-built with double walls, well insulated with clay between. He had found some old glass bottles in a pile of junk not far from the house. These he skillfully and artistically built into one section of the wall as a window to let in light.

It began freezing at night, far too cold for Peter to sleep in the wagon any longer. He was glad that the house had come together as quickly as it had, so he could at least be inside at night. It was warmer sleeping on the dirt floor than it was in the wagon, but he was impatient to get the beds ready as he found sleeping on the damp earth made his entire body ache and he could not sleep well because of the pain.

Getting hay to fill the beds meant spending several days cutting tall grass in his meadow with the big knife, then letting it cure in the sun until it was dry. He hauled the hay to his house and by tramping each layer of hay as he piled it in, he made firm mattresses in two of the beds. He covered the other bed box frames with split poles, so they could be used both as seating and storage.

When he was done filling the beds, he chopped some wood and lit the fire. It burned perfectly and soon the smell of warming earth and the musty dampness being burned away filled the home. He left the pole door wide open to let the stove draw in more fresh air to help dry the interior faster and rid it of the musty smells

He spent the remainder of the day pulling up bucket after bucket of water out of the well. The old cover had been broken and there were a lot of leaves and rodents in the water he drew up. He had made a new cover for the well, so once he finished emptying the well, the water would stay clean and fresh.

There had been a pile of dirty, very coarse, grey blankets in the bed boxes. He had taken them to the lake several days earlier for a good washing before hanging them on the spruce branches to dry. He took time that day to bring them into the dugout home and dump them on the hay beds. Their sprucey smell added to the growing freshness of his new home.

It was almost dark by the time he finished cleaning out the well. He had closed the door earlier and the heat from the stove welcomed him as he entered his home. He was cold and soaked to the skin from emptying the well with the leaking bucket. Wearily he changed into dry clothing and then spread the blankets over the hay. He stretched his tired body on the bed, just to see if it was comfortable. The warmth from the stove surrounded him and comforted his pain. He had memories of a childhood of luxury, but nothing compared to the feeling of comfort he had now, sleeping in the shelter of a dugout home on a bed of hay with warmth from a stove surrounding his weary body. He was home at last!

He had cut lots of poles and, on the nicer days, had gotten the barn built. His horse had shelter and he was ready for the cows whenever Jack would bring them. It was the last day of December when he finished the barn and the snow lay deep. He wished he had hay for his horse, but the horse seemed to be doing well on his own, pawing through the snow to the grass. Next year would be better, he thought. He had a home now. He wouldn't have to work as hard as he had the past few years and, best of all, Nataliya and the little one would be here with him. They would make some money selling cream, as Jack had said, and build up the place until he could start his dairy. His hands would have a chance to heal from the heavy work of the past few years. They had begun feeling stiff and clumsy while he was working on the railroad. Now sometimes the aching would keep him awake for most of the night. Yes, next year would be better because he would never have to work like that again. T He crawled into the blankets on the bed of hay, thankful for all he had. Eventually the pain lessened, and he slept as the New Year, 1928 began.

CHAPTER 8

There was a sorrow in those old days that can't be captured in words. When loved ones left to go far across the ocean there was the knowing that they were probably seeing those beloved faces for the very last time. Humans tend to fill the painful void with hope. As Nataliya left, she promised her mother and sister that they would soon send them money to come to Canada too. They snugged that hope to their hearts as they wept their "Goodbyes" on that day of parting, while deep inside they all knew it could be a last goodbye.

For Nataliya and Katjia, who had just turned two in January, the grief was not so deep. They were excited. Travelling by ship would be a new adventure. Little Katja seemed to understand and was looking forward to meeting the father she had never known. Nataliya could hardly wait to be with her Peter again, so it was with tears and laughter that they boarded the ship that afternoon in late March. The trip across the ocean was long and although many of the passengers were seasick, they were both spared this misery. Each new day was an adventure for the pair. Nataliya taught the little girl all the English words she knew and told her that from now on she would have to call her "Mommy" and they were going to soon see a man she would call Daddy".

They loved the storms, wind, sunsets and sunrises of beauty and, eventually, the sea birds. "When we see these birds, it means we are getting close to land", the mother told her daughter who squealed with joy.

"See Daddy tomorrow?" The girl could not hold her excitement in any longer!

Nataliya smiled and took the little hand of her daughter. "No, once we get off the ship, we have a very long train ride. It will be a few days until we get to where our new home is. Your daddy will meet us there". The little one did not understand, but she smiled, knowing that as long as her mother had her hand, she was safe, no matter how much longer the trip would take.

****

Peter was almost overwhelmed with excitement as he put a bit more wood on the fire to keep the stew simmering. This was the day his beloved Nataliya and the daughter he had never seen were coming. He had taken a bit too long in getting everything ready and now he was going to have to hurry. He did not want to leave them waiting.

Just as he was leaving, he met Jack leading three cows behind his truck. Jack stopped and called to Peter, "the price of cows has gone up so much I can only buy three cows with the money you gave me. If you want the other three, I can get them for you, but I will need more money".

Peter sat there shaking his head. He had no more money. Could they survive with only three cows? When Nataliya was there maybe she would know. He knew nothing about cows and right now he was in a hurry.

"Two of these are Jerseys," Jack continued. "Prize winning ones at that! They will give you more cream in a week than four Holsteins would in a month. And this big Holstein here. She is going to have a calf any day and you are going to have lots of milk."

"I see you are on your way to town, so I won't keep you," he rambled on. "I will just tie these here cows in your barn and bring the hay over this afternoon when I collect my tools. Just a little advice on how to take care of them. Cows can get a bit fidgety in a new place. You will have to leave them tied in the barn for a week. Do not give them even a drop of water. They must remain thirsty. Just give them lots of hay. By the end of the week they will be so calm and quiet you could sit right on them and they wouldn't flinch a muscle." With a grin and a wave, Jack drove on toward the barn.

Peter was late. Nataliya stood at the station holding Katja's tiny hand. She had not heard from Peter since he had sent her the money. She had written to tell him when she would arrive. Now there was no Peter. What if he had died? What would she do in this strange country if he never came? For probably the first time in her life Nataliya was worried and afraid. Eventually a wagon did drive up and a very tall, darkly tanned, muscular man with long black curly hair jumped down from the wagon. "This can't be Peter," she thought. "Peter is tall and slender. This man is a stranger." The stranger called her name and the voice was Peter's.

Peter got down from the wagon and looked toward the station. There was a woman and a child standing there, but the woman could not be Nataliya. Nataliya was tall and curvy. This woman was scrawny looking, and she looked much older and very tired. She wore a babushka on her head. Nataliya would never wear one of those. She would be dancing and singing with her curls flying the moment she saw him, if this was truly Nataliya. This woman looked frightened and ready to run. Not sure what to do, he called her name.

Nataliya walked slowly toward the big stranger. "Are you Peter? she asked in a shaky voice.

"Yes, I am Peter," he answered, wondering who this woman was and why she knew his name. Fear gripped him. Had something happened to Nataliya on the ship and this woman was here to bring him some bad news? Was this his little girl the stranger was holding? "Who are you?" he asked at last, his voice shaking.

"I am Nataliya", she whispered.

They looked at each other, shock written in both their faces. "You don't look like you anymore," she finally quavered.

He shook his head. "You look more like a starved baba than you look like you." He reached out and hugged her close. "Did we really think that the years and hard times wouldn't change us?" he whispered in her ear.

"Now where is my little girl?" he boomed as he scooped Katjia into his big arms. She giggled as he tossed her into the wagon and then loaded the few bags and boxes they had brought. Last of all he helped Nataliya up. She felt like a bony bird in his strong arms

Conversation during the ride to the home was strained. They had looked forward to this day for so long. Now they found little to talk about. They had nothing in common in this new land. He lived here now, and for him the old country had become history. Looking for something to say, he told her that the cows had arrived just as he was coming to the station to meet her. That is why he was late. So, they talked about the cows. Their cows. Their hope in this new land.

Her first reaction to the dugout home was a shudder. She could not imagine living in a hole in the ground with only dirt for a floor. He saw her face. "We won't live in this for very long. We can soon build a big new home."

She asked to see the cows then. She understood the care the peasants had given their cattle. These cattle were the future for Peter, herself and Katjia. She would see that they would be well cared for.

As she walked to the barn, the first thing she saw was a pile of rotting, moldy hay. "Where did this come from Peter"? She queried. "This will make the cows sick."

"Jack brought it while I was gone to meet the train."

The big Holstein stood listlessly, drool coming from her mouth. The Jerseys were in pain. Nataliya recognized instantly that the two Jersey cows had mastitis. She had helped the Healer treat cows like this many times before. It was often caused by infection from some injury to the udder, but sometimes the infection seemed to come from nowhere. Thankful that she had the knowledge and experience to be able to help the suffering animals, she set to work.

"Help me take them outside, Peter," she commanded as she untied the ropes that secured the cows inside the barn.

"No, Nataliya," he almost shouted. Jack said I had to leave them in the barn for a week and not give them any water, so they settle in." He made no move to help her.

"Peter, they would be dead in less than a week if you left them in the barn with no water and nothing but moldy hay to eat!" she exclaimed. "Who is this Jack person anyway?" Her voice was angry. "I think this man has a knife in your back! He is certainly no friend! He sold you some rotten hay and three sick cows when he promised you six healthy cows and sweet hay. He is evil! Now, please bring the other cow outside while she can still walk!" She stomped out of the barn leading one of the Jerseys.

Peter led the other out and tied her to a tree and went back for the Holstein while Nataliya searched through the boxes for the needed herbs, thankful now that the Healer had insisted she bring them with her.

First, she mixed some herbs. With Peter's strong arms to help her she managed to get a ball of the herbs on the back of each cow's tongue. Next, she filled the big pot with clean water and boiled it with another herb. After it was cooled enough not to burn the cows, she applied fomentations to the cows' udders, milking away the clotted milk after each fomentation. By evening the swelling was almost gone. She would treat them for three more days and after a week they could use the milk.

In the meantime, Katjia was squealing in delight. When Peter wasn't helping Nataliya with the cattle he tossed the tiny girl on to the horse and took her for little rides and showed her all the neat places he had found for a child to play on their farm. There were golden Marsh Marigolds growing everywhere in the wet grassy places. She came back with her arms full of the crispy flowers for her mother.

Nataliya was examining the big Holstein and soon called Peter back to help her. "There is nothing wrong with her except she has a broken and badly infected tooth," she said. "She can't eat because it hurts her too much. Can you think of some way to pull it out? I am the daughter of a dentist, but I don't think I have this skill."

They puzzled together until Peter remembered he had found a piece of thin wire lying in the junk pile. He had brought it in just in case it might be useful. "Maybe we can get this around her tooth and then fasten it to the horse. I will harness him now. Maybe we can fasten it to his collar or something."

After many tries and a mighty struggle, they got the wire around the tooth and fastened to the horse collar. The poor cow was pulled by the tooth to the length of her tether rope. For a few moments Nataliya feared the wire or the rope would break instead of the tooth coming out. Suddenly the cow made a mighty bellow of pain and the tooth came flying out. And there they stood, in each other's arms and laughing while they tried to comfort their little girl who had been watching the whole procedure and had been terrified by the cow bellowing.

Once Nataliya was done with the cows, she went to the lake and washed up as best she could while Peter watched over Katjia and checked the stew that had simmered most of the day. It was a simple meal, but hunger turned it into a feast that even Katjia ate and asked for more. Nataliya no longer felt like a stranger in a foreign land. They had a roof over their heads, food in their stomachs and each other. It might not be a dream come true, but it was their own home and their own land; a place of beginning.

When the meal was over, Peter pulled his violin from under the hay in the bed. He had not played it since he came to Canada. It needed tuning and his hands were so stiff he could hardly play, but for a time he made music like the old times. He soon lay the violin down.

They sang together with Little Katjia joining in here and there until she finally drifted off to sleep in the soft bed of hay, the music becoming part of her dreams. She already loved the Daddy that she had never seen before, and she loved her Mommy. She even liked the dirt house and sleeping on the hay was an exciting adventure.

Peter lay his violin gently back under the hay. He did not want to tell Nataliya how stiff his hands were or how they pained him sometimes. Nor did he want to tell her he would never play the violin again because it hurt too much. Instead he told her that singing with her was a greater joy than playing could ever be. She liked to sing with him and it made her happy. Outwardly, he had changed, but he was still her musical, loving, Peter.

That night Jack and Mr. Ardythe met in the bar. "Well, I don't think the Bohunk will be around much longer," Jack laughed wickedly. "We'll get rid of this one too, just like we did the last fella! I told him I would give him six good cows. I charged him enough for twelve cows, but he doesn't know anything about cattle or what they are worth. I was afraid he might get them somewhere else, so I asked him to pay me up front, that way he wouldn't have money to go looking for other cows. The guy trusted me! And he paid me for hay, too! So, I found two cows for him that had mastitis really bad. They were Sam's prize Jerseys, but he was just going to have to get rid of them anyway since they are no good any more. Sam is having no end of trouble with mastitis since he put that cement floor in his loafing barn. .He likes it since it is easy to clean but he thinks the cows are getting their udders injured. He is not too happy about all the cows that are having problems."

Jack grinned at Mr. Ardythe who was listening intently and nodding his head. "Anyway, Sam was crying on my shoulders about having to sell his two best cows for fox meat and I offered to buy them from him. I paid him a little for each cow and he was glad to get them off his hands. Then I found a Holstein on another farm that hasn't been eating. She is terribly thin and drooling all the time, I think she probably has TB. She is supposed to have a calf sometime soon, but she won't live long enough to have it. I took these sick cows out there today. I was afraid the Holstein would die on the way, that is how thin and weak she is. I told the Bohunk that the price of cattle had gone up so much over winter that there was only enough money to buy him those three cows. Then I told him to leave them tied in the barn for a week without water to settle them down. I brought him a load of moldy hay too. I got it all done before he got home from a trip to town. If he tries to milk those cows, they will kick him into the next millennium!" By now the two men were roaring with laughter.

Mr. Ardythe took a deep breath. "For sure the cows will be dead in a few days, and he will be gone. These foreigners are like rodents. Gotta keep trapping 'em before they multiply and take over my community. By the way, did he ever get that hole in the ground he was going to live in, dug? Winter came so early last fall I thought he would freeze to death before he had time to do all that digging. I am surprised he is still here!"

Jack looked a little pained. "He went snooping around his property and found where the last guy had his dugout. He cleaned it out and rebuilt it. Did a nice job of it, if I have to say so. He made a good, tidy barn too and has some pole fences up. He has been working hard, you can give him that credit to his name, but he has no money left. Without cows and without something to sell, he will either starve to death or leave. Either way he won't be your problem much longer."

Mr. Ardythe pulled out a thick roll of bills and handed them to Jack. "You are a great man, Jack. Best I ever had. You sure know how to drive the scrum out of my settlement. Let me know if they leave dead or alive. I need another good laugh.".

CHAPTER 9

When there is hope, there is also energy and direction. This was true for Nataliya and Peter during the busy first summer on their farm. The cows were well and thriving. Fortunately, there was enough green grass and they never had to eat rotten hay. The big Holstein had started eating the day after the tooth extraction, and a few days later gave birth to twin bull calves.

With the help of the horse, Peter had pulled the young poplars to prepare a large garden. With the same joy he had felt when he found the almost intact dugout home and the well, he discovered a plow buried in the grass and brush near the garden area. They planted a huge garden, rejoicing in the gift of the rich earth and the security of having a place to grow their own food.

Nataliya had laughed when she first saw Peter's bean storage can. She claimed it for its intended purpose and filled it with the rich cream she had skimmed from the milk. Every week now, Peter took a can of cream to the creamery. It never brought much money, but they were able to buy some salt, flour and a garden hoe.

Tiny as she was, Katjia would always remember that wonderful summer. There was food from the garden, wild berries in abundance, endless amounts of butter, cream, cheese and milk along with sour dough bread baked in the strange oven on the barrel stove. There was always laughter while they worked, and her parents sang together every evening even though they had worked hard all day. Every night she would climb onto her hay bed and snuggle under her scratchy grey blanket. There was no sound of wind or rain inside the cavern house. Only the sounds as her parent's sang her to sleep. Life could not have been more wonderful for the little child.

There was one serious disappointment. What Jack had said was a beautiful meadow turned out to be a marshy bog. The cows could not walk there after a rain without sinking to their bellies in the black muck. They would not eat the coarse marsh grass either, unless there was nothing else to eat. They had to have hay for winter and this coarse grass was all there would be. Nataliya, with little Katjia scampering at her heels, spent many days cutting the grass with the big sharp knife. She wished she had a scythe like the women in the old country used. It would have been easier and faster, but the knife was much better than pulling it, and risk cutting her tender hands with the sharp blades of grass. She must be thankful for what she had.

When the hay was dry, Peter threw it in the wagon and hauled it beside the barn where he made a big pile of hay. Katjia helped him by bouncing on the hay to pack it. They sang together while they worked. Only sometimes her father would become very quiet and rub his hands. Sometimes she would see him clench his hands and make a little moan as if something was hurting him.

One evening a lady walked into their yard carrying a wriggling sack in one hand and a box in the other. "Hens and two settings of eggs," she said as she handed them to Nataliya. The woman seemed uncomfortable, as if she was afraid to be there. She introduced herself as Eileen, then left without another word.

Peter was quickly put to the job of making two snug pole nests in the back of the barn. Katjia helped him fill them with hay. When it was dark, Nataliya put eggs in each nest and settled the hens on the eggs with a warning to Katjia not to go near the hens for the next three weeks.

They sold more cream and Peter bought a scythe for his wife as well as a saw, and axe for himself. Katjia had seen her mother happy before, but she seemed extra happy now as she swung that scythe and sang silly songs for Katjia as she swung the scythe through the tall grass. Before long the haystack by the barn was big enough. Now Peter spent his time making pasture fences, while Katjia helped her mother pick wild berries to dry in the sun.

To their surprise, both the Jersey cows had calves late that summer. Beautiful little heifers that looked like little deer. Katjia was thrilled and spent hours petting them until the big Holstein was given the job of raising all the little calves. They were put in a shady pasture away from the barn. The little girl was terrified of the big cow, so she had to be content with looking at the baby Jerseys through the fence after that.

When the baby chickens hatched, Katjia's little life seemed complete. They were so tiny and fuzzy that she wanted to hold them all day and would have, if Nataliya had not rescued the little things.

Yes, life was wonderful and happy on the homestead as the two young people worked toward their goal and their little daughter played and laughed and sang. It was the summer of joy to always remember.

CHAPTER 10

Jack was walking by the creamery one morning when he met Peter walking in with a can of cream. Trying to keep the look of shock off his face, Jack greeted Peter warmly, as if he was his best friend. "Looks like those cows are doing just fine for you," he almost shouted. Peter only nodded and walked past him. Jack was the last person he wanted to see.

Putting on his friendly smile he followed Peter. "So how are the cows doing?" he asked, doing his best to make eye contact. Peter put his can of cream with the others that were being shipped that day, picked up his check and left without a word to Jack.

Jack rushed to Mr. Ardythe's office. "Don't know how, but the Bohunk is selling cream," he almost shouted as he burst into the room. "I know those cows should all be dead by now. Even if they aren't dead, they wouldn't be giving milk. I don't know how they can possibly be selling cream? Something is up with this guy, and I aim to find out what is going on over there."

"I am depending on you to run this guy out of here!" Ardythe pushed his chair back and gave Jack a look that could have burned a hole in his shirt. "Let me know what you find out, but you better get the job done and get these scrum people out of the area before winter."

Jack headed for the homestead immediately. Sneaking through the woods he saw two sleek and very healthy Jerseys grazing near the barn. The Holstein wasn't with them, so Jack was content to believe she had died. He was glad she was out of the way, but these Jersey cows were his biggest problem to begin with. They were cream producers and even two of them could mean the difference between income and starvation. He cautiously crawled through the pole fence to examine the cows more closely. There was no sign of the infection.

He was sure these were the same cows, but even if they weren't, a plan was forming in his mind. Early the next morning he paid a visit to the former owner of the Jerseys. There was a handshake and Jack handed the farmer a roll of bills before he left.

Peter had taken to checking out the town dump each time he was in town. Here he found treasures that he might find useful. Wire, an old but warm coat, a sack of clothes that were still good, boots that were only a bit worn, pots and pans, children' story books, these were things that might prove useful. He had found a lot of tools with broken handles, and these were his greatest treasures. He carved new handles out of the trunks of small trees and the tools were as good as new. The list of good things that others tossed out seemed endless and Peter was a weekly visitor at the dump to see what was there.

On one particular day, he found two steel barrels with lids. Now this was a real find! It would be a place to store things like flour and beans where mice could never get them. He and Nataliya could finally stop batting over who could use the cream can! He had wanted it for storage. She needed it for cream. Happily, he tossed the barrels on the wagon and went to the store where he purchased dry beans and flour with that week's cream money. Life was not easy, but it was good. As soon as his hands felt better, he could clear even more land and they could grow alfalfa and some grain for their cows. He rubbed his hands gently. As he rubbed, he noticed some of the finger joints were red and swollen. Maybe he should tell Nataliya. She might have some potion in her herb box for this. But his stubborn pride said, "No." He was a man, not some weakling that would cave under sore hands, and expect to be babied by his woman.

Peter had just unloaded his barrels for Nataliya to clean when a police car and a truck stopped by his barn. Calling Nataliya, he headed for the barn.

"Are you Mr. and Mrs. Romanov?" queried the officer.

They nodded, wondering why the police was here, along with Jack and another neighbor called Sam. Something seemed ominous.

"Do you know whose cows you have here?" continued the police.

"They are ours," answered Peter. "I bought them from Jack last spring. They were sick when they arr...."

The officer cut him off. "If you bought these cows you will have proof that you did. Your story is not important to me unless you can produce a bill of sale and a receipt proving someone sold them to you and that you paid for them. Do you have that?"

Peter shook his head. "No, I just gave Jack the money and he brought me only half the cows he promised."

"No one would pay for cows and not have a receipt, so it appears these cows have been stolen from Sam. These are his prize Jersey cows and Jack has verified that. Sam says he has been hunting for those cows for months and asking around if anyone knew what had happened to them. Someone saw them here on your property a few weeks ago. Sam and Jack have checked it out as they did not want to believe that you people were dishonest and would stoop so low as to steal cows from your neighbors. They are definitely Sam's cows and Sam has every right to charge you with theft. Instead he has agreed to drop the charges and just take his cows back. I don't envy you right now because this is a small community. Everyone will know you are a cattle thief." He turned to Sam and Jack. "Get them out of here guys. Glad you have found them, Sam. I will be keeping an eye on these people from now on."

Nataliya spoke in her broken English, her voice trembling. "Sir," she said to the officer. "Please listen to us. Please! These men can't do this to us. My husband paid the money to Jack last fall. He promised to get us six cows. My husband trusted him to bring us healthy cows. Instead he brought us sick cows and fewer than he asked for." She was sobbing now. "We aren't thieves Sir. These are cows we bought from Jack and he never even gave us as many as we paid for."

"Prove it then lady," responded the Officer as he looked over at Jack who was grinning his innocent grin and shaking his head. "Show me the paperwork or be quiet. Don't expect me to just believe your word without some proof of what you are saying." Without another word he got in his car to follow Sam and Jack, who were leading the two little cows behind Jack's truck.

The couple stood watching them leave, too shocked to speak. Too shocked to move. There would be no singing that night.

Jack and Mr. Ardyth met that evening. "Boy, did we ever mess things up for those Bohunks this time! They will have to go now, they don't have a chance. He won't dare to even come to town anymore either! From now on they will be called cattle thieves. Somebody might just string the man up some dark night! This is just too good!" Jack roared with laughter as he held out his hand for payment.

Ardythe handed Jack another roll of bills. He laughed, but not quite the way Jack expected. Still, he clapped Jack's shoulder and praised him on a job well done. The old man had seen the family once, scraffling through the town dump, looking for anything to make their lives easier. He had seen three people dressed in rags, the woman was beautiful in a tired sort of way, the man carried himself like royalty, but it was the little girl that tugged at his withered conscience. He had never seen a more beautiful child. Now, as Jack gloated over his final crush to drive this family out, the memory of that little face flashed before him. It was so pure and innocent. Full of joy and the belief that everybody and everything was good in the world. Maybe they should have given them a chance.

He ordered another drink. He must not think this way. He had a business to run and a town to keep perfect, in his own view. There was no room for him to get soft. If that little girl died of starvation it would not be on his conscience. It would be her father's fault for coming here where he wasn't wanted.

****

Peter faced some hard decisions. It was harvest time and farmers would be hiring on extra help. He should be able to earn enough to get them through the winter and possibly buy another cow or two. But could he do it? His hands stung and ached so badly even if he was not using them for hard work. The pain seemed to have spread to his back and hips and sometimes he ached all over his body now. The thought of endless hours of pitching bundles of wheat and oats into the threshing machines filled him with dread as he thought of the pain it would cause. But he was a man, and a man takes care of his own, pain or no pain.

He left on foot the next morning. Nataliya would need the horse to bring the firewood out of the forest. In spite of his pain he had cut the trees down, but it would now be up to her to drag them out of the woods, cut them into blocks and split the blocks into pieces that would fit in the stove.

He went from farm to farm asking for work. No one would hire him now, as the gossip about the "Big Rus" being a cattle thief had spread like a plague. "We don't hire no cattle thieves," they would say and order him off their farms. One man even set his dog after Peter.

There was no work for him on any farm because of Jack's lies. No matter how in need of help the farmers might be they would not hire him. It left him no choice but to come home, hungry, exhausted and unsure where to turn or what to do next. He went to his barn and sunk his head in his throbbing hands while the blackness of deep depression took him captive.

Peter was a good man and an honest one. He trusted a person who pretended to be a friend. Because of his innocent trust, he had been cheated out of money, then stolen from and left with no visible means of supporting his family. That so-called friend had crushed out any hope he had left. He sat in his barn and cried. His family needed winter clothing. They needed a better home. They needed so many things, yet he could not provide anything for them. The little he had provided for a start was gone and he had no way of getting more. He was an ill man and could never stand the pain of working on the railway again. Sitting there with his head in his hands he saw himself as a beaten man; a failure without a future. He looked at the young chickens as they scrabbled in the dirt for food and wished he could be a chicken, not knowing, not caring, just living for the next bug they would find to eat. He could hear Nataliya splitting wood beside the dugout home. He could hear Katjia laughing and singing silly songs with her mother. He did not go to them. Even strong men cry, and Peter stayed in the barn and cried for a long time.

He had grown up in luxury. He had fled from a revolution in Russia that took the lives of relatives. When he came to Canada it had been with only one goal; to become part of the new country and raise his family to be good citizens. He had done nothing wrong, yet the one person he called friend had crushed and purposely destroyed his reputation and his ability to provide for his family. He had worked hard to get the little he had. Now it was gone, and he was seen as a criminal. His troubled mind found no solutions.

CHAPTER II

It was dark when Peter finally went to the dugout. Before Nataliya could say anything, he answered the question he knew she would ask. "No one will hire a cattle thief." He sat on the bed, the picture of dejection, with his head clutched in his aching hands.

She rubbed his shoulders. "You tried. It's not your fault. We have a home and we have a lot of food. We will not go hungry. "Did you forget that Jack and his friend Sam never thought of the Holstein cow when they took the Jerseys? They probably thought the cow had died and never knew about the baby calves. Sam should have known his cows were in calf when he sold them in the spring, but they never thought of it when they took the cows. Or else he thought they weren't born yet since the calves were all in the little pasture at the back. We have five animals now instead of just three. I shut the calves up at night and milk the cow in the morning. We have lots of milk and cheese and enough butter. That lady gave us two hens and most of the eggs hatched. We can have meat when the young roosters are bigger, and we will have eggs when the young hens are grown."

She led him to the cavern at the back of their home. "We harvested the vegetables while you were gone. Come see!"

The large cavern was full, almost to the top. She had fashioned pole bins that were heaped with potatoes, carrots, beets and turnips. Clumps of celery had been dug into the soil of the cavern. Huge cabbages hung from the ceiling along with braids of garlic and onions. Pumpkins and squash were sitting just outside the cavern along with some large pots of sauerkraut. "We have need of nothing this winter, Peter", she said as she touched his arm gently.

"There are a lot of dried peas and beans too." She smiled as she led him to one of the barrels. "Look, along with the beans you bought, this big barrel is full." She led him to the other barrel where the flour was kept. Beside the flour were other sacks filled with dried berries, mushrooms and tomatoes. "Don't worry! We won't starve, and the chickens and the little calves can have some of the vegetables during the winter too."

She took his hands in hers, noting his wince of pain as she touched him. "Don't worry," she went on. "We have two bull calves. Next year we will sell one to pay the taxes. The next year after that we will have the young cows giving milk and we can sell cream again. It will all be good again. It will just take a few years longer!"

Her words brought no happiness to him. They would have food, but she had done it all. He saw himself as useless and only a burden to his wife and daughter.

Little Katjia cuddled between them that evening, overjoyed that her daddy was home. She begged them to sing her to sleep as she slid under the grey blanket on her bed. She loved the sound of his voice. When her parents were together singing, the world was a beautiful place and she would fall asleep to the sound of their voices, knowing that her parents would keep her safe. For her and her mother it was still a time of peace and plenty in spite of what Jack had done to them. They had no idea how much physical pain Peter suffered or how deeply the events of the past few weeks had hurt him. There was no singing that night and the child sensed a sadness that had never been there before. She cried herself to sleep, not knowing why she cried.

Long after the others were asleep, Peter lay awake, his body throbbing with pain. It was steadily getting worse. "How much longer can I go on?" he wondered as he opened and closed his aching hands and tried to find a comfortable place to lay. If he couldn't work what would happen to them? Katjia would need to start school in a few more years. She would be three years old in January and the next three years had little promise of being better. What would happen to the child of a man who was branded as a cattle thief?" He finally slept in a daze of exhaustion mixed with physical and emotional pain.

It takes a brave man to admit that he is ill. Peter had struggled alone with the increasing pain for years; pretending it would get better on its own. Instead it grew more painful. The time had come to tell Nataliya. He woke the next morning, knowing he had to tell her that day. He couldn't hide it any longer. She was immediately trying to cure him, just as he knew she would. He was given nasty concoctions to drink and he had to soak his hands in hot, green water. It soothed the pain temporarily, but the joints remained stiff and swollen. There was no cure in her herb box for his illness.

He had promised her a nice home. Instead, this dugout might be all they would ever have. She told him life would go on and that hope for the future lay in the strength of their children. She shared her happy secret the next morning. In the spring they were going to have a baby. She hoped it was a boy and when he grew up, he could help his father. Even if Peter couldn't work, he could teach his son. Until then, she and Katjia would do their best, thankful for everything they did have. They had land and they could manage until things got better. In the spring, after the baby was born, she would take the plough and the horse and break up enough more land that they would not lose the homestead. They would have a secure home and a place to grow food.

****

Her pains came too soon. Weeks too soon. Nataliya rested, hoping they would stop, but they kept coming. Peter took Katjia to the barn, wrapped her in blankets and put her to sleep in the manger. He stayed with the child, his mind troubled.

Nataliya battled the waves of pain alone. She cried for her own mother as the fear of being alone to give birth overwhelmed her. When it was finally over, she cradled the tiny body of her lifeless son in her arms, breathing in his mouth, willing him to live. He lay still. There was no breath. No life. Her heart was breaking.

Peter came back after a long while and found her there, holding their dead son. She staggered to her feet, still holding the dead child, and reached for her husband, longing for the comfort of his strong arms. Instead, he roughly pushed her away from him and left.

The hurt she felt as he walked away from her without a word, tore at her very being. She thought he was angry at her for not giving birth to a strong son.

It was not anger that made him push her away and leave, but she did not know that. He was broken inside over his failure to care for her, to provide, to be a strong man. His wife should have had a doctor and a midwife to care for her but there had been no money. She had to go through this alone because he had nothing to give for her care. If she hadn't had to work so hard maybe the baby would have been born full term. He felt it was his failures that had caused his newborn son to die. He had acted in his own pain, never realizing what it did to her.

She sat, holding her son to her heart until the sun rose on that frosty February morning. She would have to bury her baby somehow, and her heart was breaking. She had needed Peter, but he had left her alone. As if in a dream she put on her coat and picked up her baby. There was not even a box to use for his little coffin. She could not dig a grave in the frozen ground so there was only the stone pile at the edge of the garden. Slowly she walked there and began moving the heavy rocks. She must go deep so wild animals would not be able to dig him out. She shuddered and cried aloud at the very thought. She held him against her and begged him again to live. She kissed the tiny perfect nose and lay his naked little body where the rocks had been. She had to put rocks on top of him now. No mother can put a rock on her baby. She wailed from the center of her being. This was the son she had loved for the past six months while he grew below her beating heart. She could not cover him with rocks and leave him there to freeze, but he had to be buried somehow. She screamed and wept until Peter finally came, and wordlessly led her to the house away from the lifeless body of her baby. He did what had to be done, weeping as he did so. She did not see his tears and her grief only made his private sense of failure grow deeper.

When Peter came inside, she was lying in the bed of poles and straw, her face turned to the wall. They did not speak. He made breakfast and went back to the barn to wake Katjia who was still sleeping in the manger under a pile of blankets. He told her the baby had died. She came in sobbing and curled around her mother. Nataliya pulled her into her arms and they wept together. Peter walked out again and did not return until cold and hunger drove him to the house.

The pain they each felt lay unspoken and unhealed. Katjia hated the silence between her parents. Sometimes she wondered if she was to blame because they didn't talk to her much either. Maybe they were angry at her too. Maybe it was her fault that all the happiness was gone. Life had changed, and the little girl suffered along with her parents.

That was the day the singing ended.

CHAPTER 12

The crash of 1929 came only a month after they lost the child. When you have no money to lose it makes little difference if the stock markets crash, but Mr. Ardythe lost his entire financial fortune in one day. In spite of owning a huge mansion and estate, he saw himself as a poor man. Many farmers owed him money, but he knew they would not be able to pay him. It would do him little good to foreclose on them, what good was more land to him now? He closed his office in town and spent most of his time in his mansion. His only daughter, Eileen, lived near him and shared the news to the community that the old man was failing in health. It was no surprise then, when news came a few weeks later that Old Man Ardythe had passed on.

What did bring surprise was that he left his huge farm and mansion plus a few quarters of unsold land, to his nere-do-well hired man. No one could remember the hired man's real name. He had been so shy and awkward around people that he had been given the nickname of "Awk." Old Man Ardythe had taken him in and given him a home a few years back. It was not characteristic of Ardythe to help the down and out, but perhaps the old man had a heart in there somewhere. He didn't have a son, so perhaps he saw him as the son he never had, although he never treated Awk especially nice. He worked him hard but as the youth grew older, Awk spent more time in the bars than he did at home working.

There was considerable speculation that the young man had been able to get the old man to change his will at the end, when his mind was confused. Concerned neighbors came to Eileen and asked her if she was going to contest the will. She just shook her head. "I was left with all the sold land to collect on, or end up owning. I have all I can handle. Right now, nothing is worth anything. I am not going to lose sleep over my father leaving something to his hired hand." So that was that. It was no one's business but Eileen's and she didn't seem to care.

On the homestead Nataliya planted a big garden that spring, just as she had the year before. She ploughed up more land to satisfy the terms of the homestead with Peter helping until the pain became too severe to hold the handle of the plough. Hay was cut and hauled. Peter helped haul the hay by driving the horse and wagon. There was no laughter, no talking and no song. It was as if part of Peter and Nataliya had died with the baby. They were each wrapped in a tomb of sorrow and guilt.

By autumn Nataliya managed to cut down enough trees for firewood and hauled them out of the forest. Peter had watched her, followed her, while saying nothing. She was irritated by his silent presence and wanted to shout at him to leave. She said nothing but worked on with silent irritation. She did not like being watched and just wanted to be left to struggle with the heavy logs without him seeing how hard it was for her to do it. If he couldn't help her, why be there?

Katjia grew tired of being with her silent parents. Instead, she spent hours alone in the dugout home, curled up in her bed and trying to read the words in the picture books her father had once found in the town dump. She hoped he would find some more and bring them home. But her father never went to the dump any more. He would sit for hours in the barn with his head in his hands just staring out the barn door.

When Katjia picked berries and vegetables with her mother, it was better because sometimes her mother would sing to her, but nothing was the same. It still felt like the sunshine was all gone. Her mother used to laugh and play games with her. She didn't do that anymore, telling Katjia she was too old for silly baby games. She did help her with English words as they worked together in the garden. Sometimes at night they read the little story books together, which was one of the happier times for the little girl who could not understand her parent's need to grieve their loss and their fear of an unknown future.

Nataliya had planned to sell the yearling Holstein bull that summer to pay the taxes, until she learned it would cost more to ship him to the market than she would get for him. It caused her no end of worry. She had heard that if they did not pay the taxes every year, they would lose the homestead. If the farm was gone there was no way of growing food. She hoped nothing would happen until she could get enough money to pay them. As for the little bull, he would become part of their food supply when the weather got cold if Peter felt well enough to butcher the animal. It would have to be done far from the house so that Katjia would never know what happened to her pet. That winter there was more than beans in the stew, but Katjia never asked what it was, and no one told her.

Another year went by. Katjia would be five the following January but the school wanted to begin a special class for four and five-year-old children, to prepare them for grade one. The program needed one more child for the program. The school superintendent paid Nataliya a surprise visit and invited her to send Katjia. Seeing her little girl's excitement, the mother reluctantly agreed to send her to the little one room school that was only half a mile from their home.

Katjia could hardly wait for September! She would finally have friends and be able to play games with other children.

Nataliya was deeply concerned about what her daughter would wear to school. There were the bags of good clothing that Peter had once found in the dump. Nothing would fit Katjia, but if Nataliya had scissors, needles, and thread she would be able to make them over for Katjia. She remembered the lovely dresses her own mother had made for her and her sister using old garments. She could do the same if she only had scissors, needles and thread. She needed soap too.

The two young Jersey cows each had a tiny spotted calf only days before the invitation for Katjia to attend school. Nataliya would be able to sell some cream again and she could purchase the things she needed to make school dresses for Katjia.

Her hopes were crushed when she attempted to sell the first can of cream and she learned it would cost more to ship the cream than she would get for it. She came home disappointed, with a full can of cream, and no soap and no sewing supplies.

In the peasant village, she had helped make soap many times using water slowly dripped through wood ashes and mixed with animal fat. Butter should work, she reasoned. Katjia watched as her mother churned the cream into butter, and then mixed the butter with the dirty looking grey water. The butter soon turned syrupy looking and got very hot. Nataliya told her this was a chemical reaction between the potash in the water and the fat in the butter. When it was well mixed the syrupy mixture was poured into a flat pan and left overnight before cutting it into little soap bars. The little girl was puzzled. How could dirty water and butter be used to get clothes clean?

"Now, wash our clothes with our new soap," Nataliya said the next morning after the bars of soap were cut. With their arms loaded with laundry they set off to the well to do the family wash with the new soap.

Katjia had once dropped butter on her clothes and it was hard to get out. She was going to have to see this soap work before she would believe it! She raced to the well. There was an old tub near the well that Nataliya filled with water, assuring her daughter that hot water would work better but there was no way to heat it so they would use cold water. Once the tub was full, she dumped the clothing in and started scrubbing the soiled spots with the grey bar. Soon there was some suds and when the garment was rinsed the dirty spots were gone. The little girl decided doing laundry was more fun when you made your own soap first.

School time was fast approaching, and the child had no shoes to wear. After she was sleeping one evening Peter brought in the dried hide from the little Holstein and showed Nataliya how to cut two squares of the hard hide, using the big sharp knife. After the squares were cut, he showed her where to cut off each of the four points as well as to cut several long narrow strips of rawhide. They placed the hide in a pan of warm water for the night to soften it. In the morning, Peter had Katjia stand on one square. He pulled one corner over her toes, the other up the back of her foot, then crossed the other corners across the top of her foot. Once everything was in place, he tied it on her foot with long strips of rawhide, then repeated the procedure on her other foot. She had to wear these booties until they dried to the shape of her feet. These were her shoes for school, and the very first shoes she had owned since coming to Canada. She was delighted with her little boots and had no idea how the hearts of her parents ached because they had nothing better for their little girl.

Black and white rawhide booties on her feet, a tattered brown dress, several sizes too large for her was wrapped around her tiny body and kept in place with a strip of rawhide; her long, curly hair was tied back with another strip of rawhide, that was how Katjia was dressed for her first day of school. The road was long and dusty, but she was so excited that she did not think of the long walk. She had anticipated this day for so long that excitement made her skip most of the way to school.

There were children in the school yard when she arrived. She hurried up to another little girl and said in her best English, "Hello. My name is Katjia . I am coming to school too and I will be your friend."

The other girl walked away without a word but a boy across the yard started yelling. "It's the Baby Bohunk, come to steal our cows! Run for your lives!" Another boy who was standing closer to her spit in her face before racing to the school house with the others behind him. She followed them to the schoolhouse because she did not know what else to do. The door was open but just as she started to enter a boy slammed the door right in her in the face and it hit her nose hard. It hurt. She sucked in her breath sharply to keep from crying. Only a baby would cry on their first day of school and she was not a baby!

The teacher greeted her cooly and showed her to a desk at the very back of the school-room. There was no one sitting beside her and she feel alone and frightened. Every now and then a child would look back at her and stick out their tongue or make faces at her.

When the teacher asked Katjia to come up to the front and try to read in front of the class there were hoots of laughter. One boy shouted, "Baby Bohunks can't read. They just steal cows." The teacher made no comment.

Struggling not to cry, Katjia lifted her chin and walked bravely to the front of the room and stood right by the teacher's desk. She read the little story the teacher handed her without making a single mistake. The teacher looked surprised to see a little girl, not quite five years old be able to read like that, especially when English was not her native language. She handed the child another book which she read just as easily. Next, she gave her a grade three book and asked Katjia to read the first page of a story. She did so with ease.

If the other children were impressed with her ability to read, they didn't show it. Instead, they had seen her booties while she was standing in front of them, and she walked back to her desk through a lot of snickers and a loud shout of, "Yee haw! Here comes Rawhide! Bet she stole and skinned a cow herself. She helps her pappy that way," echoed through the school room.

At recess time she did not go outside, but at lunch time the teacher demanded that she go out. The teasing continued the minute she was in the school yard, so she walked to the swings as far away as she could get from the other children and sat down. Suddenly she was hit from behind and went flying off the swing to the ground. A big boy, the one named Nate, was standing over her, roughly jerking the rawhide strips from her hair and trying to pull the booties off her feet while shouting. "You're just a cow thievin' Bohunk. Whose cow ya' wearin' anyway? We hang cow thieves, so we are gonna' hang you."

Just as suddenly as she had been knocked off the swing, another of the big boys grabbed Nate and sent him rolling on the ground beside her. "Leave her alone!" he shouted as he stood over the boy on the ground. "You should be ashamed of yourself, hurting a little kid like her. Now get up and get out of here."

Kneeling beside the little girl, he took out his handkerchief and wiped the blood from her cut lip. "Are you OK?" he asked, as he lifted her back to the swing.

She nodded her head, determined not to cry, but a few tears were in her eyes anyway as she looked up in his face. "Why are they so mean to me," she asked, her voice quivering.

"I wish I had that answer," he said as he helped her to her feet. "I don't know why some people are mean, but from now on, no one will touch you because I am your friend." He looked at her booties. "And from now on your name will be Rawhide! You are strong and tough like Rawhide, so it fits you. Be proud of who you are and be proud of the name they called you." He helped her to her feet. Even dressed in her ragged clothes he thought she was the most beautiful child he had ever seen. He vowed to himself that no one would ever hurt his little friend, Rawhide, again. Awkwardly, he tried to tie her tangled curls back in the rawhide strips.

The piece of homemade cheese and bread she had brought for lunch was lying on the ground, covered in dirt from the scuffle. "Are you hungry?' he asked as he handed her an apple and a sandwich. It was the first apple she had ever eaten. It was so good she even ate the core. The sandwich was filled with something sweet and something creamy and brown. She had no idea what it was, but it was good. She wished she could have more of whatever it was, but she was too shy to ask for another sandwich.

When the children began playing games, he led her over to the group. No one was making fun of her anymore. They stood silent, looking at the big boy. "This girl is named Rawhide, and you will never call her anything else," he spoke loudly enough they could all hear. "She is my special friend, so none of you can ever make fun of her or hurt her again." He glared at Nate and spoke to him directly. "Do you understand? Now tell her you are sorry."

Nate looked at his shoes as he mumbled something that sounded a bit like,"Sorry."

A game of baseball was just beginning, and the big boy made sure she was included. She ran in with the others when the bell rang and started to go to the desk in the back. Instead the big boy whispered, "Come sit in the desk beside me." He motioned to the empty desk. A few moments later he handed her a piece of paper where he had printed, "You are Rawhide. I am Johnny. I am your friend and I will never let anyone hurt you."

She sat there and looked at him with her beautiful smile. The things the others had said and done to her did not make her feel so bad any more. She had Johnny for a friend now, and she was safe. Her lips were swollen and bruised, and her knees and elbows were scraped but she felt so happy to have a friend that the pain did not feel so bad anymore.

When school ended, he caught up to the little girl as she started down the road to her home. "I am going to walk with you, Little Rawhide," he said, taking her tiny hand in his, "just in case there are any lions or tigers on the road."

She looked up at him, her deer-like eyes filled with fear. "Are there lions and tigers here?" she asked as she remembered stories in her little books at home.

"No," he laughed. "But I live close to you and so do some mean people. I just want to be sure you are safe, Little Rawhide. I will walk to school with you every day from now on if that is OK with you."

She smiled happily. He was her big hero from that day on!

CHAPTER 13

The depression years did not hit that farming community as hard as many other areas were hit. Johnny's mother, Eileen, Mr. Ardythe's daughter, had taken over his accounts after his passing. She was a deeply caring person, as different from her father as summer is from winter. When she was left to manage her father's accounts, she knew immediately that no one would ever be able to make even their interest payments until there was a different financial climate. They got very little for their produce and the payments set by her father were high. Knowing that leaving things the way they were would be to drive people from their homes, she made a policy that they need only pay what they could afford until things got better. Eileen was their lifeline during the Great depression. Johnny was like her and his father Frank who was also a kind and compassionate man. He possessed the same caring nature as his parents and at school he was the undisputed leader.

In spite of Eileen Carpenter's compassion toward the debtors, there were still hardships. Soon the other children had lunches as plain as those that Rawhide brought to school. No one made fun of her rawhide shoes any more. She was accepted as part of the group and included in everything. She was four years younger than Johnny but n spite of the age difference they were the best of friends. Through the years she became known as "Johnny's girl" as well as "Rawhide".

He continued to walk her to school and back and eventually he shared his biggest fear for her safety. She had to walk past the mansion of a house where Awk lived. This house used to belong to Johnny's Grandfather. Johnny didn't trust Awk or what he might do to Rawhide, if he saw her alone on the road. He was afraid of Awk himself, but his need to protect this little girl was stronger than his own fear of the weird man.

Sometimes Awk would be staring at them over the fence when they walked by the house. The look on his face made her shiver and walk closer to Johnny. Like Johnny had told her, "He isn't ugly to look at, but he has an ugly look."

****

The years went by rapidly for Rawhide. At school she was the star student and a good athlete. At home she worked hard to help her mother with the heavy farm work. The little heifer calves had grown up and had calves that had calves and so the herd slowly grew to ten cows. Once again there was cream to sell every week. It brought little income, but when you have no money at all, just a little seems like riches. Nataliya was able to purchase things like scissors, needles and thread. She saved pennies until she could buy a scrub board and a thing called an iron that heated on the stove. Rawhide no longer had to go to school looking quite so poorly dressed. Homemade, yes, but not ragged and un-ironed. She even had shoes to wear as she got older, although Johnny always told her he liked her rawhide booties better.

The silence between her parents had ended, but the happiness they had once shared had not returned. They were two hurting people who did not communicate their pain to each other. Nataliya felt Peter had rejected her because she had not given him a son. Peter felt like a failure. They could have healed each other's hearts if they would only have talked about their pain and listened to each other. Instead they hugged their pain to themselves and trudged through life together, growing older in a sad union. Barred from society in the community by race prejudice and the falsehood that branded them as thieves, they were outcasts without friends.

Peter continued to spend many hours alone in the barn, angry at himself and the world around him. Slowly, the once tender-hearted man changed into a complete stranger to his family. He began blaming Nataliya for all their troubles. It was for her that he had ruined his hands working on the railroad and on the farms. He was a musician and if it hadn't been for her he still would be one. He thought of his violin and cried over his inability to play it any more. *If only I hadn't come to that little Ukrainian village and fell for that peasant girl*, he thought bitterly, *My life would be better and I wouldn't be ill"*.

Nataliya had given birth to another stillborn son while Rawhide was at school. Her mother wouldn't talk about it, but days later Rawhide found a tiny grave marked with a cross of wood tied together with rawhide strips. She sat beside the little grave in silent sadness. She wondered if her mother had named her baby brothers. Someday she would ask her mother, but now she just slipped back into the home and circled her with a hug. They cried in each other's arms.

Peter started taking the cream to town again, and before long he went back to his weekly foraging in the dump, hoping once again to find things that might make their lives easier. He had always felt a need for music and one day, hearing music as he walked past the bar on his way back from a quick trip to the dump, he decided to go in. It was a song he knew. He sang along with it, ignoring the insults the men were shouting at him. The men soon grew silent as his beautiful baritone filled the room. When the song ended there was some clapping and cheering mixed with the insults. Someone kept setting drinks in front of him. He knew they were laughing at him, but the more he drank the less he cared what they called him or how much he hurt emotionally and physically. He went home drunk and slept it off in the barn. When he woke again he felt worse about himself. He craved more whisky to numb all the pain again. He began using the pitiful little cream cheques to buy whiskey, leaving nothing for the family. Nataliya soon realized what was happening and took the cream to town herself after that, collecting the cheques and giving Peter nothing.

He began spending most of the time in the bar, singing for whatever liquor the patrons would give him. It became a pattern. Go home drunk. Sleep it off in the barn. Feel worse than before, and then try to get drunk again.

Not everyone accepted him. Most made fun of him, but he did make friends with a man they called Awk who was almost always there, drinking and gambling. He taught Peter how to gamble even though Peter had no money to gamble with. This made Peter lie awake at night wondering where Nataliya hid the cream money. If he had that money, he could win at poker games like Awk said he did, and they could all have a better life. He searched many times while she was out milking but could never find her money stash. He became even more sullen, depressed and detached from his family.

As time went on Nataliya showed signs of breaking under all the stress she was enduring. Out of necessity Rawhide had to share more and more of the farm duties. Hard as it was, it was training ground for the unknown future that lay ahead for her.

CHAPTER 14

It was 1941. Rawhide had celebrated her fifteenth birthday that January and Johnny had brought cupcakes to the school for all the children to celebrate her birthday. Later, as they walked down the snowy road toward Rawhide's home, he handed her a brightly wrapped package and asked her to open it. Inside was a pair of soft white angora gloves and a scarf to match. She stroked them against her face and tears started falling.

Surprised, Johnny stepped back. "What is wrong, Rawhide," he asked, his stammering voice registering shock at her reaction. "I have never seen you cry before. Don't you like them? I can take them back to the store and get you something different."

She looked up at him with tears streaming down her face, but she was laughing at the same time. "Johnny, I love them! I have wanted white fuzzy gloves or mittens like the other girls all have! I have wanted them for so long, but I knew I could not ask my mother to buy them for me. I didn't dare let myself think about very much, but I still wanted them so much! I am so happy that you gave them to me that it made me cry!"

Johnny didn't understand how this girl, who had taken so much hardship in her life without shedding a tear, was crying now, over soft fuzzy gloves, but his heart sang as he looked at her tearful, laughing face.

She reached for his hand and gave it a squeeze. Thank you so much! I love you, Johnny Carpenter."

His heart could not have been fuller! He loved this girl.

The one-room school that Rawhide attended did not teach beyond grade nine, so this was her last year to attend the little school. Anyone who wanted to get more education must either study at home by "correspondence" or leave home and attend a boarding school in the city. Rawhide's best girlfriend, Charlene would be leaving in the fall. It was their last day of school and the girls chatted in the school yard while Rawhide waited for Johnny. He had finished grade nine, four years before, but he still walked her to school and back every day.

As they waited, Charlene shared her dreams. "I am going to be a doctor eventually. I don't want to stay on the farm forever. I have had enough with smelly old cows!" She stamped her foot for emphasis. "What are you going to study to be?"

Rawhide envied her. "If I could, I would study to be a lawyer. In reality I will probably end up still living in a house with a dirt floor and helping my parents survive until I am ninety."

Both girls laughed. "Actually, you are going to marry Johnny and live happily ever after. You will have ten daughters and send them all to school wearing rawhide boots," grinned Charlene.

Rawhide laughed. "As long as they have a father like Johnny, no one would dare make fun of rawhide boots!"

The girls hugged goodbye as Johnny entered the school yard. "Until we see each other again. Good luck," they said in unison as Charlene headed in the opposite direction toward her home.

Johnny gave her his usual warm smile. "Do you think your Mom will mind if you are a little late doing your chores tonight?" he asked as they started down the dusty road.

Rawhide laughed. "I pretty much do them all myself, so if I am too late, I am the only one who will be unhappy. My father will be too drunk to care where I am, and my mother will probably be resting. She does a lot of that now."

Johnny led the way down a grassy path until they came to a large field. Beyond the field were grassy meadows and trees. She followed him to the trees where a pile of lumber lay. "Sit down," he said, motioning to the pile of lumber. Sitting beside her, he began. "Most people don't know this, but before my grandfather died, he gave me the title to a very large tract of land. What you see here is only part of it. I am going to build a home here, and this lumber is just the beginning." He paused and reached for her hand.

"Rawhide, I have loved you since that first day you came to school in ragged clothes and rawhide boots. I was this little rich boy who had always had everything I ever wanted. You came to school dressed like that because you had nothing else to wear. Other girls would have pouted and cried and probably not come to school unless they had the nicest clothes, but you came the way you were with your little head held high. Even when they teased you and hurt you, you never cried. I could see you fighting back the tears, but you held it together. That took real courage! I fell in love with you and those little spotted booties that day and you have had my heart ever since. You have always been one brave, beautiful and kind girl. I dream of you being my wife someday, so I can always protect you from the lions and the tigers."

They laughed at the old memories of their school years together, but Johnny had more to say. "I think we feel the same way about each other. I know we are both a bit too young to get married, but I am asking if you will wait for me. I have joined the army because I have to do my share to protect the freedoms of others. I will be leaving the day after tomorrow. This war started in 1939 so it can't last too much longer if enough of us join up to fight. I will be back soon. Don't worry!"

Tears filled her eyes. "I love you Johnny Carpenter, I always have, and I always will, but please don't go to war. I would marry you tomorrow if you would promise not to go," she pleaded.

He held her hands, "Little Rawhide, there is no ocean big enough, no enemy strong enough to keep me from coming back to you. I made you a promise on that first day of school that I will always take care of you and I will keep that promise."

"You can't promise me that, Johnny. Soldiers die, and if you do, death won't let you come back to me. Why do you have to go?"

He was quiet, looking at the western sky. Finally, he spoke. "I have to go to fight for the freedom of your people and of mine. Yes, I might die, but that is the risk I am willing to take to do my part in this war." He reached in his pocket and brought out a small package with two rings inside. Her name was engraved on one, his on the other. He handed her the one with his name on it. "Take this ring, Rawhide, wear it on this chain, next to your heart. I will do the same with this one. When I come back, we will put these rings on our fingers at our wedding. I will come back to you. Just believe I will and think positive."

They stood, holding each other and crying as they kissed that first wonderful kiss. There was an aching in her heart that their first kiss could also be their last. They held hands as he walked her home, but there was little to say. It was too soon to dream because the spectre of war loomed between them before they could ever be together again. They did not kiss again because he said their first kiss was sacred, one to hold in their hearts as a memory until he returned from the war.

"Maybe I will have to swim the ocean and fight the enemy to get you back again, but if I have to do that,I will," she whispered as they said goodbye.

He walked away. She watched him until he was out of sight, trying to believe he would be coming back, but sad thoughts kept smothering the hopeful ones she sought to focus on. She tried not to think of him lying dead in the battlefield, but she couldn't help it. Soldiers were dying every day and he was going to be a soldier. Grabbing the milk buckets, she cried the entire time she was milking the steamy cows.

Johnny left two days later along with several other local boys. His parents were in the crowd that gathered to say "Goodbye" to the boys. When they noticed Rawhide, they came to stand beside her. Eileen slipped her arm around the girl's waist. There were no words. Only the mixture of fear, sadness and hope that triggered tears as they waved to their loved one. People seemed to understand, they came to give her hugs, invite her over sometime; all the things people do after they accept someone. She was very much a part of the community. She was Rawhide, Johnny's girl and Johnny was everyone's friend.

She watched as he boarded the train. He turned and waved and then he was gone. The haunting sound of the train whistle brought tears, her life seemed as empty as the train tracks now were. Life had changed and there was no turning back.

On her way home, Rawhide went back to Johnny's property and curled up on the lumber pile to think. Mostly she thought about her parents and the unfair treatment they had received in this community. They lived there in that dirt hut, separate from everyone because of race discrimination, poverty, illness, unjust treatment and falsehoods that ruined any reputation they could ever have made. No one came to see them. No one invited them for a meal or to be part of any of the get-togethers that farm communities are famous for. They were lonely and alone.

She was their daughter, yet very much a part of the community in general. There were few who did not know and respect the beautiful Rawhide. The only difference between her life and the life of her parents was the way they had been treated. They were rejected for no fault of their own.

Right from the start, Johnny had made her believe in herself, had included her in everything, but most of all had been her friend. He was always there if she needed to talk. She wondered if it would be the same without him or would she just become another shunned member of her family. The thought frightened her.

CHAPTER 15

Rawhide attacked the work on her parent's farm with vigor. She hoped hard work would help her to worry less about Johnny. She had learned to swing an axe like a woods-man. Her mother was not feeling well and able to do less and less. It became Rawhide's job to cut trees for firewood as well as put up a winter supply of hay for the growing herd of cattle. She was happy that her parents had bought a mower to pull behind the aging horse. She did not have her mother's skill swinging the scythe nor did she want to learn. The mower could cut more in an hour than her mother could cut in a day. Her mother helped her haul the hay to the barn, but not with her former bounce and energy. The woman seemed exhausted.

Although she did not have a chance to go to boarding school as Charlene had done, Rawhide was determined to finish High School. She enrolled in what was called "Correspondence School' in August." She was delighted when her books and lessons arrived in the mail. She could hardly wait for the heavy summer work to be finished so she could continue doing school work. She loved the challenge of learning and secretly wished she could go to University as Charlene planned to do but was well aware of the reality that this could never happen. Charlene's parents could afford to send their daughter for an education. Hers could not and she accepted the fact, but still let herself dream of what she wanted.

Her father rarely tried to help with anything but, sat brooding in the house or barn when he was not in the bar or sleeping off a hangover. There was a contrast between her parents. Her father had sunk even deeper into a depression that summer. He could see no way out of their situation. His constant companions were a sense of hopelessness and the burning pain of his illness; his hands so swollen and red that he could do little more than feed and dress himself. In contrast it seemed her mother had always worked vigorously until this summer, content to ensure their daily needs were met without showing concern over lost dreams. Now, she looked tired, older than her years and a bit bent over from the hard work. Rawhide could remember her mother being beautiful. As she watched her walking heavily in a pair of oversized rubber boots, a soiled torn dress hanging unevenly to her boot tops, and rough, blistered hands carrying firewood, she wondered where that beauty had gone.

She was with her mother, digging potatoes from the soft garden soil when her father returned from town one afternoon. To her surprise he was not drunk but seemed excited. Laughing as if he had rediscovered hope, he asked them to come to the house and talk. Rawhide dropped the hoe she was using and followed her mother to the dugout. Seeing her father so exuberant meant the news had to be good. She felt tingles of excitement as she sat on her straw bed to listen to what he had to say.

Her anticipation was dashed instantly. Peter told them that his friend Awk was the hired man that Old Man Ardythe had left with houses and lands. Awk was wealthy beyond belief. That morning Awk had driven him to one of the farms that he had been given. There was a beautiful home, big barn and other outbuildings. It was ready to move in. The land was rich with grain fields ready to harvest and pastures waiting for cows. If Rawhide would marry him, he would give all this to her parents immediately.

Rawhide gasped in horror and jumped to her feet in an instant. "I will never marry Awk," she almost screamed as she bolted out the door. She went back to digging potatoes with energy triggered by her rage. What could her father be thinking to even consider this? She remembered being "Daddy's Little Girl." Even though he was ill, in pain and often drunk she still loved him and saw him somehow as her protector. What he was asking of her now was cruel and unacceptable. *How could he even think of considering this*, she stormed to herself as she flung potatoes in the large bucket.

Her mother soon joined her. "Rawhide," she began, "Please do this for our sake. You are our daughter and it is your duty to obey your father and care for your parents." She started to cry. "I promised to help my own mother and bring her to Canada. I got so busy trying to make this place work that I never kept my promise. I could have done something else. Maybe got a job somewhere so I could have sent her the money. But no, I just didn't do anything for her because I was selfish. I haven't heard from her for years. I don't know if my mother is dead or alive. I know now that people have starved to death over there, and there is war. I never helped my mother out of there, and I grieve for what I didn't do to save her. You have a chance to help us, and not feel the guilt I have for not caring for my mother when I could have."

Facing her mother, Rawhide shouted, "I said I will never marry Awk and I won't." I don't love him, and I could never marry a man I don't love. I love Johnny and as soon as he comes back from war we will get married and then I can take care of you and my father."

Her mother snorted. "Love exists only in the imagination of silly teenage girls. You don't know if you love Johnny or not. You are too young. Besides, he will either die in the war or forget all about you and come back home with another girl on his arm, while you have wasted your life waiting for him. As your parents, it is our duty to get you married off. This man has money, so you will have a good life and it will give us a life too. We need a strong man in the family and it will be good to have Awk to help with the heavy work your father and I can't do."

Her words cut Rawhide to the heart and she started to cry. "Am I nothing but a cow to my parents, to be traded off for some land?" she cried. "Is having money more important to you than I am? You don't know who Awk really is. He is a drunk and a gambler. I will never marry him, not for you, and not for anyone else.".

Grabbing her daughter's hand, the mother cried out, "Please Rawhide. Please listen! This is a chance for a better life for all of us. Your father is too sick to work, and I can't take any more of him being drunk and depressed. I feel too tired to go on any more and a young girl like you should not be doing all the heavy work you have to do. The only hope we have is for you to marry Awk. It is your duty to help us when you can."

Rawhide walked away, leaving the potatoes laying on the ground. She did not return to the home that night, choosing to curl up in the haystack instead. She thought of running away, but she knew her mother was expecting another baby even though she had not been told. She couldn't abandon her now. She would just stay where she was and help her parents all she could. They could not force her to marry Awk.

Strangely nothing more was said. There was no silent treatment and life went on as normal for the next few weeks. Each time her parents went to town she waited eagerly, hoping for a letter from Johnny. She had written him, telling him everything that had happened. Didn't he care enough to answer or had something happened to him already? She shuddered at the thought.

Her mother had saved enough money to buy a wagon load of oats for her cows as the poor slough grass did not have enough nutrition for the winter months. They got the grain from a neighbor who would chop it up for them and put it in bags. Usually Peter went for the grain and unless someone was there to load the wagon, Rawhide went with him. That morning, her father felt too ill to get out of bed, so he told Rawhide to get the grain for her mother.

It was a short drive to the Bailey farm where they bought the oats. Mr. Bailey was not in the yard as she expected he would be, but she skillfully backed the wagon into the barn, sure he would show up in time to help her load the grain. To her surprise Awk was inside the barn. "What are you doing here," she asked quickly, fear almost choking her.

"Old Bailey couldn't be here today, so he asked me to load for you," he responded with an evil smirk on his face.

It did not take long for him to load the bags of oats, but just as she was going to climb into the wagon, he grabbed her wrist. "Marry me," he demanded.

"Awk, let me go! You are hurting my wrist!" she shouted. "I will never marry you. I would rather die than marry you!"

He grabbed her, and she fought with every ounce of strength in her body. She bit him and kicked him until he seized her long hair and threw her backward. Merciful blackness came as her head struck the wall behind her. The next thing she knew, she was lying naked in the wagon, the horse was heading down the road on his own and her clothing lay in a heap beside her. Reality of what had happened washed over her and with it came a flood of hatred. She hated Awk for what he had done to her, but she hated her father more. He had planned this for his own gain without a thought of her. How could the Daddy she had once loved, turn into such an uncaring, unfeeling lump of inhumanity?

Her father was in the barn when she got home. She never said a word but threw the heavy bags of oats into the bin as if they were feathers. She knew her father was watching her. She wanted to scream at him, call him every name she could think of and hurt him as badly as she was hurting. Instead she silently walked away as soon as the job was done. The hatred toward her father kept boiling. She knew she could not live in the same house as he did, no matter how much hardship her leaving would cause her mother. And what of her mother? Was she part of this evil that had been done to her as well?

She walked to the highway, hoping someone would give her a ride. She knew hitchhiking was filled with danger, but so was living at home. She walked and walked but no one stopped. The sun was setting, and it would be dark soon, but even if she had to walk all the way to the city she would not go back home.

An older gentleman finally stopped and asked her where she was going. She shrugged, telling him just to drop her off anywhere in the city, she had no address. He wouldn't accept that. "Can't just drop a little girl like you off on the street. I will take you to my daughter's house for the night instead. She will help you find where you are going."

His daughter came to the door and took in the situation quickly. This was another runaway farm girl hoping to find work in the city, she guessed. Still, this girl seemed different. She was a beauty, but she seemed frightened, desperate as if she was running from something bigger than she could handle. She took her inside and ran her a warm bath. Perhaps in the morning she could get the girl to talk, but it was too late tonight.

Rawhide had never had a tub bath before. The luxury of the hot water soothing her hurting body was the most wonderful thing she had ever experienced. She loathed to come out, even when the lady insisted that she had been there long enough and needed to get some sleep. A silky nightgown was waiting for her and the lady led her to a room with a real bed and real sheets. The soft quilt snuggled around Rawhide as she slid under it. She had never slept on anything but a hay bed with coarse grey blankets for covers, nor had she ever had a pillow. *Is this how other people live?* she wondered as she finally drifted off into a troubled sleep, filled with nightmares that woke her up screaming.

Morning brought more new experiences, like toast and peanut butter. "Peanut butter?" Now she had a name for what was in that sandwich Johnny had given her on her first day of school. She vowed when she got a job, the first thing she would buy was a jar of peanut butter. She was not left to eat in peace though, since the lady had many questions to ask her. Far too many for Rawhide's comfort. She assured the lady that all she needed was a job and a place to stay. Perhaps if she had shared her story the lady could have helped her in some way, but she couldn't talk about it.

The kind woman gave her suggestions as she drove her to the city center. There were many shops and restaurants with "HELP WANTED" signs in their windows. At first, she was excited, believing that she would be hired on the spot, but by late afternoon she was feeling desperate. No one would hire the shabbily dressed girl who so obviously knew nothing of city life. She had never been to the city before and had never shopped for anything. She had no idea how far she walked that day, but her feet ached, and her big breakfast was now only a distant memory. The good smells in each restaurant she had entered to apply for work only made the hunger pangs worse.

She passed another restaurant with a "Help Wanted" sign and walked in with little hope left that she would be hired. This restaurant was a rundown spot in a less than posh neighborhood, yet to a girl who had grown up in a dirt dugout it seemed quite luxurious.

She was hired almost instantly and told there were rooms above the restaurant she could rent. The best part was that it would be taken off her pay at the end of the month, so she could move right in. She could start work immediately as soon as she changed her clothes. "I have nothing to change into," she stammered, her face flushed. "This is all I have."

The manager, a tough looking older woman clucked her tongue and looked at her for what seemed like hours. At last she said, "I needed a waitress, but I guess we can use you out back to wash dishes until you can buy something decent. She was shown a giant stack of dirty dishes. "Ya do know howta' wash dishes I hope?" she said as she showed her where soap and tea towels were. Many hours later the woman showed her to her tiny room. A narrow bed with a bare mattress was on one side of the room. A small dresser with a mirror on the other side. Nothing else.

Wondering how she would keep warm in the chilly room Rawhide asked, "Is there a blanket or something I could use?"

The woman shook her head. "Got nuthin' like that here, but guess this here is better'n sleepin' on the street this time a' year. So here's yer key, n' the bathroom is just down the hall. Be at work at 4:30 sharp in the mornin'. Think ya might be good for more'n washin' dishes, so you get to help with the cookin'. My name is Elsie, so don't be calling me Ma'm."

As the girl shivered through the night in the chilly room, she thought of the barrel stove and the coarse blankets in her home. At least they kept her warm. She was eager for morning to come when she could go back to the steamy kitchen.

She did her best to comb her hair with her fingers like her mother used to do and then braid it into a fat braid. Deciding she looked as good as possible she hurried downstairs.

Her boss surprised her a few days later with a package containing a pair of stockings, a couple of dresses, a pair of shoes and a hairbrush. Then she combed the girl's hair, twisted it and pinned it into a very flattering upsweep and sent her out to wait tables. Rawhide was delighted as the pay would be a bit better and she got some generous tips; enough to buy a blanket. Life was good, but it was not to last!

Three weeks later a wave of nausea hit her as she carried food to one of the tables. Quickly setting the food down, she raced for the bathroom. Her boss followed her. "If you are sick you had better take the day off. Can't have you scarin' away the customers like this!" Thanking her boss, she went to her room and lay down. She felt worse in the morning. She did not go to work. That afternoon her boss came to see her. "Stuff is goin' around, she said. "You better take the rest of the week off."

Monday morning, she felt no better. The boss came up once more. "Are you pregnant"? she asked bluntly. "Can't have no pregnant girls pukin' it up in a restaurant."

"I don't know. Maybe I am. An awful person raped me," she wailed miserably. "That is why I ran away. My father arranged it to try to force me to marry this guy. Please let me stay here and just wash dishes or something. I have no other place to go."

The woman patted the girl's shoulder. "Pregnant girls can't be workin' here, but I have a friend that c'n help you. She c'n give you steady work n' a place to stay too after she takes care of that bun in your oven." Rawhide had no idea what she was talking about, but a job and a place to stay sounded good to her.

The woman took her to what seemed to look like an ordinary house. They were met by an older woman with a lot of color on her face and jet-black hair. "So, Elsie, what do we have here?"

Elsie pushed Rawhide forward. "Girl here got herself in the family way and is needin' some help and a job after. She is a real looker, so she will sure boost your business." She winked at the other woman and left.

Rawhide was soon hurried up the stairs where the woman began to explain the procedure and the expectations of the job. The girl listened in horror realizing the kind of help she was going to get and the job she would have after. Her friend Charlene's mother, who knew all about everything, had told the girls about places like this that sold the girls bodies for a price. She had also graphically pointed out how many girls die every year from what she called, "knitting needle infection." In a panic, Rawhide fled down the stairs and out to the street as fast as she could run. When she was too tired to run, she walked and walked some more on that frosty November day, with nowhere to go and no idea where to find help. Sometimes she would go inside buildings and try to warm herself until someone would ask her to move on.

Eventually she passed an office with the sign., "Smith and Sons, Legal Firm." Maybe a lawyer could tell her who to turn to for help. She walked inside, thankful for the blast of warm air that met her.

One of the lawyers agreed to see her and listened as she poured out her story. "How old are you, child", he asked, rubbing his chin.

"I am fifteen," she answered. "But I will be sixteen in January."

"Well, you do have some options. There are homes for unwed mothers and I could probably arrange for you to go there. I would need your father to sign though, since you ae under age and there would be charges he would have to pay."

"What are charges?" she asked

Your father would have to pay some money to send you there. Do you think he can do that, or be willing to do that?"

She shook her head.

The lawyer continued. "Your other choice is to marry this guy and make the best of it. From what you have told me your father wants you to marry him and this guy wants to marry you. Sounds like he is well off as well. Right now, with so many men off to war it sounds like you have a great opportunity here, not only to be a "well to do lady," but help your parents out as well. So if you have any smarts at all you will go home and get married to this gentleman before you freeze to death on the streets."

Without another word, Rawhide got up and left.

The lawyer cradled his phone in his hand. He hated to do what he had to do but this child was in grave danger on the city streets. He dialed the police station. "Fifteen-year-old runaway headed in your direction. Female. Her name is Rawhide Romanov. Good looking kid. Wearing a blue cotton dress, brown shoes and a brown sweater. She told me where she is from and what her father's name is. Contact me if she will not give you the information personally."

"There is a Missing Persons bulletin out for this girl already. Boyfriend or whoever he is, got in contact with the police a few weeks back. Thanks," was the response.

The wind had picked up. Dry leaves scuttled over the sidewalk and snow was beginning to swirl with the leaves. Rawhide pulled her thin sweater around her and walked faster. She had only walked a couple of blocks when a police car pulled up beside her. The Officer got out and asked her name. "Rawhide," she shivered.

"I am going to take you down to the station where it is warm," he said. "A child like you can't be wandering around the city with no place to go on a night like this."

Thankful to be out of the biting wind, she crawled into the warm car, even though she feared the police would contact her father. Her only choices were to run off in the cold and freeze to death or face whatever the police decided to do with her. The stress of the past few weeks numbed any hope of freedom she had once had. She had little emotion left except a need to be warm.

Once in the station she was treated with hot chocolate and cookies. She had never tasted hot chocolate before and had no idea what it was, but it tasted even better than peanut butter and bread. Hit with a wave of nausea,she threw it up in minutes. A few minutes later, a lady showed her to a cell that had a bed in it. It was a place to stay at least.

She was so cold, tired and ill all she wanted was rest. She pulled the blanket over her and went to sleep.

In the morning her father and Awk were there along with a Judge. There in the police station, with two officers as witnesses, feeling ill, trapped and rested enough to feel desperate, the frightened child agreed to marry the man she knew as Awk. That was the first time she knew he had a different name than Awk. Now she was Mrs. Harold Belker, wife of a man she hated, daughter of a man she hated and trapped into going back with them. Her world had crashed around her.

The ride home in Awk's car was long. The smells of gas and oil made her nausea worse. She told them she was sick and asked to be let out. They wouldn't stop and instead handed her an empty lard can. They drove to her parent's place to let her father off and then Awk took her to his own place, threw the key at her and told her to go in. He drove away without a word which was the only good part of her day.

She was intimidated by the very size of the mansion, but with nothing else to do she wandered from room to room looking at the exquisite furnishings. There was what seemed to her, a house below the house and another one on top. In the house below the house, that she would one day learn was a basement, she found a huge heater stove. There was a small pile of wood beside it. She put more wood on the fire and went back up to search through the rest of the huge house. The house on top of the house had six bedrooms with beautiful quilts and pillows. One bed was rumpled and very dirty. Awk's bed! She shuddered and quickly closed the door.

There was a big pantry off the kitchen but there was no food except for three little soda crackers which she quickly devoured.

Although it was still early afternoon, she chose a bedroom as far from Awk's as possible and locked the door behind her. The bed was soft, covered with the finest linens, the quilt felt like puffy clouds should feel. She cried herself to sleep, wishing she was a tiny child again, sleeping on the hay bed with her mother and father nearby, laughing and singing. Everything was so safe then. Would it ever feel safe again?

CHAPTER 16

Awk was not there in the morning. By now she was weak with hunger and wondering desperately what she could eat when there was a knock on the door. Eileen and her husband Frank came in with some boxes and bags and a wonderful smelling casserole. "Just thought there might not be much in the pantry," Eileen said cheerily, as she set down her parcel and gave Rawhide a hug. "Awk always eats in town so we were pretty sure there would not be much here. Did he give you any money? We could take you to town for groceries if he did."

The girl shook her head. "He didn't leave me anything. Thank you so much for the food though. I am so hungry. All I have had in the last two days was breakfast, and only a cup of hot chocolate and three crackers since. I didn't know what to do to get food here before I starved." She sniffed the casserole. "Would you find it rude if I ate some of this right now, in front of you?"

"Go ahead, dear girl. That's what I brought it to you for! We will just sit here with you and keep you company while you eat." Eileen began dishing some food for the girl as she spoke.

After Rawhide had eaten her fill, Eileen seated herself on the sofa and pulled the girl down beside her. "I don't know the whole story here, but I am guessing some of it. I know that you have been forced to marry Awk and you are expecting his child. The neighborhood gossip has told me that much. Frank and I want you to know we live just a quarter of a mile away, and we both have a telephone. I will show you how to use it. Do not be afraid to ask us for help. We will try to convince Awk to provide you with food, but if not, we have our eyes on you and won't let you starve."

Shortly after they left, Awk came home and asked her to come and walk around the farm with him. Not wanting to, but afraid to say no, she pulled on her thin sweater and followed him. He showed her a herd of Hereford cattle grazing in the dry, yellow grass. "Every morning I want you to throw down some of this hay for them." he demanded. "If there is snow you will have to feed them more and throw down some of this straw too, for them to sleep on. This is going to be your job from now on and you better do it right."

She wanted to ask why he didn't take care of them himself, but unsure of how he would take that, said nothing. Instead, she asked for money for food. He didn't just refuse to give her any, he jumped around and yelled, "Earn your own money or starve to death, I don't care which, but I'm not feeding you. You are useless to me. You're nothing but a worthless Bohunk!"

 He crawled into his soiled bed and slept until evening. Then, without a word of where he was going, he got in the car and left again. After that he seemed to come and go as he pleased. When he came home he would always check to be sure she had fed his animals correctly and then come in, yelling insults at her. She was always glad to see him leave but, out of fear tried her best to do everything he demanded of her while he was away.

A week later her father was at her door, angrily waving a piece of paper. "This is useless," he shouted. "I went to get the title to the land Awk gave me and he doesn't even own it. He lost it in a gambling debt and someone else has the title." He angrily threw the transfer papers Awk had given him, to the floor and demanded, "You have to come home right now. Your mother is sick, she can't take care of the animals any longer and you have to do it for her." He reached as if to grab her hand and force her to come with him.

Jerking her hand back she shouted, "I will never go back there! I was a good daughter and worked very hard for you until you traded me off like a cow for a piece of land that doesn't exist. I no longer consider you my father. In fact, I never want to see your face again! Now leave this house and never come back!"

Her conscience pained her immediately. She knew her mother wasn't well. Rawhide had spent her life being a caring and helpful daughter, trying to spare her mother as much heavy work as possible. She quickly thought of a way to help her without going back to the homestead.

Her father was still within calling distance, so she called him back. "Bring the cattle here and I will take care of them for Mother. You need to bring the hay and any grain that is still there as well." Her father's shoulders slumped. "I can't do that alone and you know it! You will have to help me if I have to bring them here. I told you, your mother is very ill, and she can't help with anything."

"If you want it done, get your dear, chosen, son-in-law, Awk, to help you, because I won't." she responded. "This is the only way I will help, so it is up to you to get them here." She closed the door to block out anything else he might say to her.

The next day the cattle arrived with Awk smiling from ear to ear as he drove them into the yard. She had never seen him smile before and wondered if chasing cattle was that much fun for him. He was still smiling as he hauled the hay. He even helped her get her mother's cows into the huge dairy barn without yelling and cursing at her. As soon as the job was done, though, he left and did not come back for weeks.

Rawhide spent the next two weeks caring for all the cattle. There was a milk room in the barn with a cream separator. Frank showed her how to use it. It was so easy compared to having to skim cream off of cold milk and by the end of the week there were four big cans of cream to sell. Her father came to pick it up and she demanded he bring back proof he had given the money to her mother and bring her back a few dollars to buy her own food. That was all she would ask.

She had been cleaning the big house from top to bottom when the thought crossed her mind that she should bring her mother to this big house. She pictured her mother sinking gratefully into those puffy quilts. Her mother could have her baby here and Eileen would be there to help her. She herself would be there to see that her mother rested and had food.

She had only walked a short distance toward her parent's place when all the angry thoughts came back. Her mother had not defended her. In fact, she had wanted her to marry Awk and maybe she was party to the scheme as well. She hadn't even come to see her since she came back from the city. Then, the worst thought of all worked its way into her mind. 'If her mother came, her father would have to come too." She had ordered him out of her house, and she would not let him stay. She wanted nothing more to do with her father. Her brief burst of compassion ended, and she ran back to her house.

A week later her father came to her door, holding a tiny bundle wrapped in a coarse blanket. He was sobbing. "Your mother had the baby this morning. Before it was even born, she started screaming that it was dead. By the time the baby was born she had gone into some kind of a trance and I can't wake her up." He handed Rawhide the squirming bundle.

She carried the tiny one inside and looked at the face of her baby brother. Looking at her father she asked, "What did you name him?"

"Your mother wanted to call him Alexander if he lived, so I guess that will be his name. Now I need to get back to your mother."

Rawhide made a quick call for help to Eileen, who arrived in a short time carrying bottles, diapers and baby clothes. Seeing a question in the girl's eyes she said, "Oh this? I just never got rid of Johnny's things," she said as she placed the items on the kitchen table and chose some tiny garments to dress the baby.

Milk was boiled and quickly cooled. Eileen curled up in a big chair to feed the little man while Rawhide watched and learned.

Frank came in a little later with blankets and a cradle. Eileen tucked the sleeping baby in to the cradle while giving Rawhide more instructions and a promise to come back and help with bathing in the morning. "Call if you need me in the night," she reassured the girl as she left.

With neighborly concern Frank and Eileen then headed their car to the Romanov place. It sounded as if Nataliya was in desperate need of some medical help. Peter met them, trying to bar entrance to the humble home. "We are here to take Nataliya to the hospital," said Frank as he pushed past Peter and walked to the bed where she lay.

"You can't take her to a doctor," shouted Peter. "We have no money. If I would have had money don't you think I would have taken care of my own wife?" he asked bitterly. "Now get out and leave us alone!"

Ignoring his outburst, Eileen went to the side of the sick woman. "Don't worry about money right now, Peter. She needs help, or she might die," Eileen spoke up from where she was stroking the woman's forehead. "Just help us carry her to the car. You are coming too, because you both need help."

It took some time before Peter agreed to go with them, but at last he slumped into the seat where Nataliya was propped and pulled her head onto his shoulder.

Frank brought the chickens to Rawhide the next day. "Your parents are both in the hospital and may be for a long time. You have enough to handle with this little brother of yours and your own little one does not need you overworking. I am going to take care of the chores, at least until Awk decides to come back and look after his own. The boy has a family. It's time he grew up and accepted some responsibility."

Eileen stood smiling down at Rawhide as she sat cradling her baby brother. "You are just a natural at this you know. Born to be a mother!"

The girl looked up with tears streaming down her face. "I almost brought my mother here and then I got this angry feeling inside and didn't. If only I had, none of this would have happened and she would be here, and everything would be fine". She was sobbing now. "What if my mother dies? It will be my fault."

Eileen sat beside her. "Yes, it would have been nice for your mother to have been here but stop beating yourself up. There is more wrong with your mother than a nice house and a warm bed would fix. Maybe it had to be this way. Now both your parents will get the medical help they need, and we will see how things go from here."

Rawhide handed the baby to the older woman. "I just feel so terrible though. I can't forgive my father for destroying my life. I can't stop hating him. I hate Awk too, for what he did to me and now every time he comes home, he just yells at me and calls me names."

Eileen sighed. "I had a hard time forgiving my own father so I understand what it feels like to hate. I have had my own struggles with this.

Your father is from Europe where it was not unusual for the father to arrange a marriage for a daughter. They look for future for the daughter that would help the entire family as well. That is probably what he thought he was doing. Your parents were desperate, and this may have seemed the only way to make a better life for all of you. They are both ill and probably more desperate than you or I can understand. Unfortunately, your father got taken in by Awk who promised him a home and a way to make a living.

You have been badly hurt, yes. What happened to you was cruel and evil. You have every right to be angry, but you are not destroyed unless you let it destroy you. You are doing a great job here, taking care of Awk's cattle and your parent's cattle. If Awk yells and criticizes you, he is the one who has failed, not you. My son Johnny always said you were as tough as Rawhide and now I believe it. The best advice I can give you is let go of the anger and let yourself heal. Never give up! You have an entire life time ahead of you. If you dwell on the wrongs that have been done, that is what will destroy you. Keep your mind busy by planning ways of making your own life better. That is how you will move forward and stay sane." She gave the girl a one-armed hug. "Now, let's go bathe this little guy."

A few days later she left the baby with Eileen and went to her parent's home. Concerned that dampness and mice would ruin her father's beloved violin she took it home with her, along with her grade ten books and assignments from the correspondence school.

Once she was back at her own home, she opened the violin case to check for any moisture there might be. To her surprise a bundle of letters addressed to her fell to the floor. They were from Johnny. Fresh anger against her parents came over her like a tsunami. They had hidden Johnny's letters from her! They had lied and said he never wrote her. She read them all. His last letter ended, "No matter what happens to you, no matter what happens to me, I will always take care of you, my little Rawhide. Be strong!"

Eileen found her weeping, surrounded by the letters when she brought the baby back.

She wrapped her arms around the weeping girl. "This is a terrible time to have to bring you sad news. I got word today that Johnny went missing in action somewhere in the South Pacific during The Battle of Pearl Harbor."

Locked in each other's arms they sobbed together in their agony; the raw grief of a mother grieving her only child, and the grief of a girl, too young to be embattled with what life was handing her, weeping for the one who said he would care for her forever.

CHAPTER 17

The winter crept on. With Frank doing the chores she had a lot of spare time on her hands. Since she could work at her own speed, she finished Grade 10 by April and began Grade 11.

Pushing herself to do as much schoolwork as she could, helped to keep her mind off Johnny during the day, but she grieved when she should be sleeping. Why had he gone to war? Going MIA only a few months after leaving home could not have made any changes in the outcome of the war so what was the point of him going? She remembered how he had looked that day as he asked her to marry him. He had held her in his arms, his curly hair blowing in the wind and smiling that wonderful smile of his as he promised he would be back.

Through the terrible months that she had endured since Johnny had left, she had kept a dream alive that he would soon be home to rescue her from the miserable situation she was in. That dream had died with Johnny and she was left with the stark reality that he wouldn't be back; she was going to have to make sense of her own scrambled life alone. Education could be her way of escape, and escape was her goal. She studied with the tenacity of a drowning woman who has been thrown a life preserver.

Her other pastime was exploring and cleaning every inch of the huge mansion. She discovered a hidden stairway to the attic and being curious, she climbed the stairs to see what was up there. The attic was spacious and nearly empty, but at one end was a small room with a padlocked door. Someone had left the key in the lock and although she felt a little uneasy, she opened the door and looked in. At one end was a very small window. Mats on the floor, and a quilt showed that someone had slept in there. "A child perhaps?" she wondered, when she saw a little red truck sitting in the corner. She noticed a bump under the quilt and bent to check it out. There, to her surprise was a small cardboard box filled with money. Delighted with her find, she took it downstairs and counted it, thrilled to see there would be enough for her to buy feed for the cattle and take Little Alexander to a doctor and have him checked out.

She had known almost from the start that baby Alexander had some kind of health problem. He was not growing well and always had a blue color around his mouth and nails. Rawhide worried about her little brother endlessly. Now she could afford to take him to the doctor and hopefully get some medicine to make him well and strong.

The Doctor examined him and shook his head. The little boy needed heart surgery. He wouldn't die immediately without the operation, but he would never be well and strong until his heart was repaired. The sooner the better. It would be very expensive, but she set a goal to save all the money she could toward getting him the help he needed. She was comforted to know what was wrong and there was hope for him once she could afford the surgery.

Awk had not been home for weeks, but in his usual way he just walked in, criticized her for not getting more work done and demanded food. While she was getting some food ready for him, he went to the attic. He came down furious and demanded the money back. She told him she had spent it on medical bills and cattle feed. Awk had no control of his temper. He beat and kicked her until she fell to the floor. Then he was gone, leaving her lying semi-conscious on the floor, his car tires squealing as he sped out of the yard.

She staggered to bed, covered in bruises from head to foot. When Alexander cried out in hunger, she managed to get him a bottle and lay him beside her to feed him. She wondered how her own baby was after the beating and suddenly realized she didn't care. It was Awk's child, conceived in violence. She didn't ask for this child; didn't want this child, and she had this haunting fear that it would be like Awk.

Eileen found them there a few hours later. In grave concern she called the doctor. After examining her he reported that, although the girl was badly bruised there were no broken bones and she would be fine in a week or two.

Frank came by an hour later with news he had heard in town. Awk had gotten in a fight in the bar. Details were scarce, but things had not gone well for the other man and Awk was in jail. Rawhide spoke her mind. " I hope he stays there forever and never gets out."

Eileen tenderly stroked the girl's hair, a look of deep sorrow on her face. "My hope is that he gets some help somewhere. He's human too", was all she said.

It was a was a warm afternoon in July when the pains started. Eileen came to stay with her and care for Alexander. The pains tore at her and she was angry. Angry at the pain. Angry at her father. Angry at Awk and somehow all that anger was channeled toward the little being struggling to leave her body. The baby was causing her pain like she had never experienced before. She screamed to Eileen that she did not want this baby and begged her to take it from her and never let her see it.

Things were not going well, and the doctor was called to provide the assistance the baby needed to enter the world. Shortly after the doctor's arrival, a tiny person added his own little voice to the adult voices around him and wailed with hearty lungs!

"You are one strong girl, Rawhide," smiled the doctor as he handed the baby to Eileen. Now you have a beautiful baby boy that looks just like you! Congratulations! What are you going to name him?"

"Just take him away! I don't want him. I don't even want to see him!" cried Rawhide, turning her face away and refusing to look at her baby.

After cleaning the tiny boy and wrapping him snugly in a blanket Eileen sat beside Rawhide. "There has been enough hate and hurt in this family already," she said gently. "This little boy didn't ask to be, and he is innocent of anything that happened to you. Awk didn't ask to be born either, but I think if he would have had a mother's love, he would not be the way he is. Just because this is Awk's son it does not mean he will be like his father. Who he becomes is mostly in your own hands, Rawhide. I know you are a loving person. Don't deny your love to your little son. Right now, he needs his mother to touch and hold him. He had been through just as much as you have, and he is little and scared and lonely. Comfort him!"

Grudgingly, Rawhide finally looked into the face of her son. Eileen's words, "He didn't ask to be born," struck a chord inside her. This child was not an extension of Awk but a tiny, innocent, helpless, little being. If it was Johnny's son, she would have wanted him and not fought the waves of pain the birth had caused. This baby had not been wanted, but like Eileen had said, he was not to blame for anything. She finally held out her arms and Eileen gently gave the baby to her.

His soft little body cradled against his mother and as he did an immense wave of love for her baby engulfed her. She stroked his tiny arm and whispered, "Hello Robby. We are in this mess together, but I promise to be the best Mommy that I know how to be."

Eileen stayed to help her for the first week and found every opportunity she could to cuddle the babies, especially tiny Robby, but Alexander got his share of cuddles too. The rocking chair that Eileen had brought over when Alexander was born, was put to work with all the rocking and cuddling.

"You will make a wonderful Grandma someday," Rawhide said, as she watched Eileen bathing Robby one morning. The moment she said it, Rawhide wished she could take the words back. Johnny was gone. Eileen would never be a Grandma.

A look of sadness crossed Eileen's face as she responded, "I will just be Grandma to these two little boys for as long as they want to be spoiled and Grandma'd."

For a moment Rawhide wished her own mother could be with her too. She hadn't though of her mother in months. Some of the anger she felt toward her parents changed to concern. Was her mother even alive? She wondered if she would ever find out what had become of her parents.

CHAPTER 18

The road back to health for Nataliya was slow. She was still young and her will to live was strong. After many months of rehab, she was declared healed with no aftermath of the stroke she suffered. A kind nurse had found her work in the hospital kitchen and a little apartment nearby. Things were going well for Nataliya, but there was a segment of her life missing. She had been told why she was brought to the hospital and she remembered she was expecting a baby. No one could tell her what happened to the baby. Where was Peter? No one seemed to know. Where was Rawhide? There were no answers to the questions that whirled in her mind as she tried to reconnect herself from the missing parts of her past to the present

She hired a ride to visit her farm and Rawhide once. She cried with joy when she learned that Alexander was her own son and worried like any mother over his heart condition. She wanted him to be with her but decided she could not keep him and work as well. It was wiser to leave him with his sister and his sister's own child. The two little boys were already inseparable.

There was an elderly custodian working at the same hospital where Nataliya worked. She had often seen the man walking through the hospital corridors, loading garbage and mopping floors. There was something about him that was oddly familiar, as if she had seen his face in a dream and had forgotten the dream but not the face. They passed each other in the hall day after day, smiled and said, "Hello," and went on their busy ways, and she wouldn't think about him until she saw him again.

Her biggest concern was not who the custodian was, but where Peter was. She had followed so many false leads to locate him and was about to give up when someone told her there was a big man named Peter in home across the city. She had a free day from work and called a cab, her heart pounding with the hope that this time she would find her husband.

The cab driver was none other than the custodian who quickly explained that he did not have an identical twin, but he did have two jobs. As they rode along, her eyes caught a name on the visor. "Ivan Burak." She knew this was her father's name but was that this man's name or had someone else put that name up there?

She made conversation about the weather, the state of the war; anything but ask him if he was her father. How could she ask an almost total stranger a question like that? Ah yes, she could ask him where he was from.

She cleared her throat nervously. "Where are you from originally, sir?" she queried.

He looked at her for a while and as he gazed at her, he suddenly felt like he was looking at a younger picture of himself. Same dark curls, same mischievous smile, same cleft in the chin, same dimple on the left cheek. Finally, he stopped staring and spoke. "I came from the Ukraine. I lived a number of places in there, but the last place I lived was in Kiev. And you?"

"My mother came from Kiev. She was born and raised there. I was born there as well, and my last name was Burak. My father was Ivan Burak". She looked back at him. Their eyes locked in a mixture of disbelief and hope.

"Are you Nataliya?" He pulled to the side of the road and brought his car to a sudden stop as he asked the question.

She nodded, unable to speak.

"Where is my Olena, then? Is she here? And your sister. Where is she?" His voice was husky with emotion

"She is probably still in the Ukraine, if she is alive. I haven't heard from her for a long time. They had a terrible famine over there. The last time I heard from her she asked if there was any way I could help her. Stalin was purposely starving the peasants to get them off the farms and thousands were dying. She said that she and Anicha had left the village where we had lived. They were trying to find somewhere to go, but they were just wandering the last I heard from her. Now with this war there is no hope of communication even if they are still living." Nataliya had tears in her eyes. "I had hoped my husband

and I could send her money to come to Canada, but it never worked out that I could. I feel so guilty."

They shared stories as they drove along. He described how he escaped the soldiers. She told of her mother taking the wrong road and how they ended up living in a little peasant village. There was so much to talk about.

He came into the care home with her as she searched for her Peter. They found him sitting in a corner, staring out the window. With a cry of joy, she rushed to his side. "Peter, my Peter. I thought I would never find you again. I have been searching for you for so long and I began to think you were dead."

He held out his arms and they were both sobbing. "I thought you had died and that I had lost you forever," he whispered. "I am sorry for so much hurt I made for you. I think of our beginning and how we sang together. We had so much happiness once."

She took his sore hands in hers, stroking them gently. "You have suffered so much. We both have. That was not our dream when we were young either but maybe we can begin a new life." She smiled a little. "I went out to see Rawhide and our little son, Alexander. Thank you for giving him that name. He is not strong and needs an operation on his heart, but he will be fine after that. He looks just like you Peter! We finally have our son! We have a fine healthy grandson too! His name is Robby."

Peter looked down, shame and pain written on his face. "And Rawhide? How is she?"

Nataliya sighed. It has not gone well with her, but she is doing all she can to survive and care for the little boys. Awk is in jail. Rawhide was happy to know I was alive and well, but beyond that, I did not feel she was happy to see me. She was very cold toward me and I do not blame her for that.

We tried to gain land. Instead we hurt and lost the only thing we ever had, our daughter." Nataliya was weeping by the time she finished speaking and she saw that Peter was sobbing, his great shoulders shaking with the weight of his shame and grief of what he had done to his daughter.

Although the visit was short it was an emotional time for Peter and Nataliya while they shared their sadness and memories of happiness. The vist culminated in forgiveness and a determination to spend the rest of their lives together.

Ivan Burak looked on, still in shock that his grown daughter had just walked into his life again and was getting a glimpse into the life she had lived. He invited her to move into his home to share expenses and she joyfully accepted the invitation. As soon as she could arrange Peter's discharge from the home, he joined them. There were many evenings spent sharing more stories of all those years of life that they were apart.

Puzzled by Ivan's choice of employment Nataliya questioned why he worked as a custodian instead of Dentistry. He explained that to work in Canada he would have had to go back to university for a year and then write a big exam in English before he could get a license to practice. He had no money to do so. He had taken a job cleaning a school, so he did not get paid much. Most of his money went for rent, a little left for food and only a little to save toward the studies. He was studying English, feeling that soon he would have enough money set aside for university and understand enough English to write the exam.

His hopes were dashed when the war of 1918 broke out and he was sent to a camp as an alien. Once the war was over the university would no longer accept him because of his "record". He had no choice but to spend the rest of his days as a custodian. He had eventually saved up enough to buy a car and drove taxi as well. "That is just the life I have to live," he said. "And I am thankful for what I have."

CHAPTER 19

The good news on that beautiful morning in May of 1945 was that the war was over, yet that news brought a heaviness to Rawhide's heart. Johnny would not be among the other young men that came home. Nate, the school bully, was the first one to come back. She struggled with dark resentment. Why should he be spared, while kind hearted, caring, Johnny had lost his life? It seemed unfair.

Awk was out of jail, but he was not allowed to be in town. That did not mean he could not come back to his own home, but so far, he hadn't. Frank and Eileen had rented out their farm and retired to the city that spring. Rawhide began making solid plans of her own. Without Frank's help she could not care for the boys and the growing herd of cattle. Worse than that, she lived each day in fear that Awk would return and beat her again. She would be leaving as soon as she could get all the arrangements made.

She had saved all the money she could toward Alexander's surgery, but it was not enough. There was a large herd of two-year-old Hereford steers as well as six more from the milk cows. If she sold these, and the milk cows there would be enough money to pay for the surgery and a bit left over for living expenses until she found a job. She would leave Awk all the cattle that had been there when she came, plus the yearlings and baby calves so he could not accuse her of theft. He would have more than he had when she came. It was summer, so they were out on pasture and would not be needing much care. Hopefully some of Awk's cronies would let him know before winter that he needed to take care of his animals himself.

Frank and Eileen had a basement suite they would let her live in, rent free, until she had a job. In two more days, the trucks would be coming to pick up the cattle. Alexander's surgery was slated for the following Monday. Rawhide was looking forward with eagerness to helping her brother, as well as having a better income to care for the boys.

She was busy packing their few belongings when she heard several trucks drive into the barnyard. They were two days early and she was not ready for them to come. Taking a little boy in each hand she went out and saw one of the trucks backed up to the cattle chute, loading the milk cows.

These were not the trucks she expected, and the Sheriff was parked beside the truck, watching as the milk cows were loaded. She could see a couple of men on horseback bringing the rest of the cattle in from the pastures. She approached the Sheriff. "What is going on here? I didn't order these trucks."

"Wasn't your job to order the trucks, lady. These cattle are being picked up to settle your husband's gambling debts." the Sheriff responded gruffly.

Rawhide stood in shock. "Sir, the milk cows and their calves belong to my parents. This is my only source of income plus I need milk for my children. They can't take these!"

"These beasts are on your husband's land, lady. They all belong to him no matter where they came from. I sympathize with you, but you have no rights at all here. The man's debts have to be paid. In fact, if you had sold any cattle you would be charged for theft because they belong to someone else. There is nothing you can do here. Get back in the house with these babies before someone gets hurt."

"Then please. At least leave me one cow so I have milk for the boys," she pleaded.

He turned from her to watch the loading. "Can't do that lady. All the cattle have to go, unless you have the money to pay for them."

Unsure what to do next she led the little boys back to the house. The exertion of walking left Alexander winded, the blue color deepening around his lips and nails. She wept in anguish for her little brother. Would there ever be another chance for him to have that surgery and be a healthy and active boy, like little boys have a right to be? This was all so cruel and unfair. She vowed she never wanted to see another cow. They seemed to be easy pawns in the hands of dishonest people.

The farm yard was empty and desolate. Without the cattle there was no longer a reason to stay there. Frank and Eileen were away on a trip across the border and would not be home until Sunday night when they had planned to get her and the boys. The plan had been for Eileen to care for the boys while she worked, but that plan was made with the assumption that Alexander would be a healthy little boy after surgery. It would be asking a lot of Eileen to care for a weak, sickly child as well as a mischievous active one. Rawhide knew they would do it, but it seemed wrong to burden down the older couple who had done so much for her already. Yet right or wrong there was not another choice to make.

Before the week was over there was a knock on her door. Two men and a lady were there with some papers in their hand. "We have brought your husband. He has cirrhosis of the liver and is dying. There is nothing more than can be done for him. We don't know how much time he has left but we can't keep him in the hospital any longer unless you can pay for it. He has asked to be brought home to die."

Rawhide stood as if glued to the floor and tongue tied.

The lady spoke again. "We are going to carry him in now. Where do you want us to put him?"

Her mind spun. He would have to be downstairs in the smaller room off the parlor since the main bathroom was downstairs. She led the way to the sofa in the smaller room. "Put him here," she said, patting the sofa. By the time they had carried him in, she had blankets and pillows, making a temporary bed. She would have to bring a bed down from upstairs later, but for now he had a place to rest.

She gasped as they carried him past her. This bloated, orange/yellow person looked nothing like Awk. "Are you sure this is Harold Belker?" she asked incredulously.

"Yes, Ma'm. His papers are all here in this envelope. You can check it out for yourself if you have to, but this is Harold."

Making sure the little boys were safely out of the way she carried the bed down, piece by piece and set it up next to the sofa where Awk lay. It was a struggle to help him to the bed once it was ready and an even bigger struggle to get the sofa out of the room by herself. She was exhausted and flopped down on the easy chair in the room. Awk had been watching her wordlessly while she worked. Now he spoke. "Why would you do all this to make me comfortable? I expected you would ask them me put in the barn where I deserve to be."

She couldn't answer him. Why had she done this for him? He was right. She could have just put him out there to die and go on with her plans to move to the city. Someone might have found him there long after he had died, but he would have died alone, cold and uncared for. She shuddered. She would not even let a stray dog die that way. It didn't matter what he had done to her, he was a hurting human and she would care for him as best she could. She went to the kitchen to warm him some broth.

Rawhide had learned well from her mother and had a huge garden. She had the savings that she had put away toward Alexander's surgery to live on, so she knew she could manage for a while.

Perhaps it was the good food she gave him, but Awk was soon able to get up and walk around a little. This eased her burden of care. What surprised her was his tender attention toward his little son. She had never thought of him being anything but cruel and selfish, yet with Robert in his arms she saw another side she could not believe existed. For the two months he lived, he read to Robby every night and played with him when he felt well enough. Once he even managed to climb the stairs to the attic and brought down the little red truck and gave it to the little boy.

One evening, after the boys were sleeping, he called her to the parlor where he was resting. She sat across from him in the great armchair.

"Rawhide," he began, "I am dying and we both know it, but before I die, I want to tell you something. I am Eileen's son. Yes, I am Johnny's brother, or at least half brother."

She stood to her feet. "You are fibbing," she shouted. "How could you make up a horrible lie like that?"

Shaking his head, he went on. "I am not fibbing. Eileen told me the part of the story I didn't know. It is the truth and before I die you need to know it is the truth for Little Robert's sake. Please sit down again and listen."

"Her mother died when Eileen was only thirteen. She had been close to her mother, but never got along well with her father, so after her mother's death, she spent a lot of time on her own. Her father hired a young man named Jack, to be his manager that summer. Jack was a charmer. With that smile of his he soon had the lonely girl infatuated with him. It didn't take long before she was pregnant with his child. When she told him, he refused to acknowledge that he was the father. In fact, he went to my grandfather and told him she had been running around at night with some boys from town and was now pregnant."

At the name of Jack, she sat bolt upright. Jack? The same Jack that cheated her parents was Awk's father? She felt bile rising in her throat at the thought that her own little Robby was the grandson of someone as evil as Jack.

Awk went on. "Mr. Ardythe was my grandfather, although I can't think of him as a grandfather. He was a man who would never accept any disgrace or blot in his family, so he built that little room in the attic just to hide his daughter away. He kept Eileen locked in there until I was born, telling anyone who asked where she was, that she had gone to live with an Aunt in Toronto to finish high school. He delivered me himself and then, leaving me in the care of Jack, he took Eileen to the Aunt's place. Her father told her to stay there, and said that on pain of death she was to keep her mouth shut and never tell anyone about the baby. This so-called grandfather of mine kept me hidden away in that little room for years. Only he and Jack knew of my existence, except for my mother, Eileen of course. He and Jack made up a last name for me and registered me as Harold Belker."

Rawhide felt sick to her stomach at the thought. No wonder Eileen said she had trouble forgiving her own father.

"Eileen never came back to the community until after she had married Frank and had Johnny. My grandfather gave them that nice big farm close to this house where he lived. When I was twelve the old man took me out of the room just before Christmas and told everyone I was a foundling that he took in. Of course, he was praised for being such a caring man to take in this orphan. I will never forget that Christmas. Little Johnny got piles and piles of toys. I had never had a toy in my life and I nearly cried. I hated the little guy because he was so loved while I had nobody. His mother was kind to me and kept making sure I got extra treats. I liked her from the start and wished she would take me home with her, so I could have a mother like that. I didn't know then that she WAS my mother. The old man soon sent me back to my room. I lay there feeling hurt and angry. I didn't understand who I was or even what a family was, but I had gotten a little glimpse of something I had never had, and I wanted it. I had almost cried myself to sleep when the kind lady came up to the attic and gave me a toy truck. I was so thrilled to have a toy of my own. Then she kissed me on my forehead and quickly left as if she was afraid to be found there."

After that I saw this kind lady and her little son quite often. I loved her but I hated that little boy. He was so cared for and got so much that I had never had. Most of all he had that kind lady to love him and all I had was an old man that made me work hard and was never very nice to me. He never allowed me to go to school. When I was old enough to be in the community on my own, I did not know how to act toward anyone. That is why people started calling me Awkward. It hurt so bad because I wanted friends and I wanted to fit in, but I had no idea how. I don't know how to explain how I felt. I wanted something that I could never find, and I had this big empty feeling inside me. I still do."

His voice was getting hoarse. Rawhide rose to bring him a glass of water. "Go on," she said as she seated herself back in the great chair. "How did you find out Eileen was your mother?"

"I was cutting brush beside the road when she walked little Johnny to school one day. I was sixteen. Johnny was seven. She asked me to be there when she returned so I waited for her. That is when she told me that I was her son and told me her father would never let her acknowledge me. She told me how sorry she was that she hadn't let everyone know she was pregnant and made sure she would have help to be able to keep me, but she was still a very young girl, ashamed of the pregnancy and terrified of her father. By the time she was allowed to return there was no way of erasing the years of damage done to her baby. Her father refused to let her take me unless she would lie and say she had adopted me from an orphanage. Eileen refused to lie, but still terrified of the old man, she just let things slide, hoping it was the best choice for all concerned. She did not tell me Jack was my father until after the old man died."

Awk closed his eyes, exhausted. He opened them as she rose to leave. "No, please stay a little longer. There is more." He struggled to find a more comfortable position.

"Jack had always sort of made me feel like I was his little buddy. He could make everybody trust him, I guess. Sometimes he would bring me a little of what he called happy juice and give it to me with a wink. It tasted funny. I didn't like it, but I wanted to please Jack, so I would drink it while he laughed at me for choking. By the time I was a teenager he was bringing me a lot of happy juice and I was hooked on it. When I drank enough, I didn't care if anybody liked me or not, or worry about what I did to others. When I was old enough, I started going to the bars with him and drink and gamble. It seemed like the only place I was ever accepted."

"When I think back, I realize Jack egged the men on to see how drunk they could get me and then it was usually him that beat me at gambling and took my money or anything I had that he wanted. He would drag me home to sleep it off and laugh and laugh at me for being a fool in front of everyone."

People were surprised then, when Old Ardythe died he left me so much money and property since it was obvious to all I was the neighborhood drunk. The truth is the old man had no part of leaving that to me. Jack somehow managed to change that will without the old man knowing about it. Jack knew that eventually he could get everything for himself if he kept me drunk and gambling."

Awk took another sip of water and rested for a moment before he continued. "Eileen came to me and told me it was my chance to be the man I was meant to be, not a drunken boozer. That is when she told me Jack was my father and begged me not to trust him. I did stay sober for a while, but Jack kept asking me to come to the bar with him. I was lonely, so before long I was back where I was before, hating myself for being weak, but wanting to drown out all my loneliness and pain."

"As I told you, I always hated Johnny. I used to see him walk with you to school and back. You were the most beautiful girl I had ever seen, and of course Johnny who had everything, had you for a friend too. Every time I saw you together, I got angrier and angrier because I felt it just wasn't fair. I could see how you looked at me and I knew you were afraid. When you grew up you were even more beautiful. Everyone knew you two were in love and I vowed to hurt Johnny even though it would mean hurting you. When he went to war, I finally had my chance. When you wouldn't marry me, I raped you just to hurt my brother."

Rawhide sat with her head in her hands. She had innocently become part of a tangled mess of lies and treachery and she had suffered because of it. Her mix of emotions overwhelmed her. "Is there more?" she asked.

"Yes, a little. Jack was the one who took the cattle. I gambled and lost to him. He has the title to all the land that was ever in my name as well. He is letting me stay here and call it my home for as long as I live but as soon as I am gone, Jack takes over. There is nothing for you, and you will have to leave as soon as I die."

There were tears in his eyes now. "Rawhide, I don't know how to tell you how sorry I am. I wanted to hurt my brother, but I never hurt my brother. The war took him, and he never came back to the mess I made of your life the way I hoped he would. Instead of hurting him, I destroyed the life of the most beautiful woman I have ever met. Can you ever forgive me?" He was sobbing now, his bloated yellow face contorted in pain, both physical and mental.

Rawhide sat silent for a long time. A mental picture of a tiny boy spending his childhood locked away in an attic dungeon, longing to be part of life; wanting to be loved even though he had no idea what love was, flashed through her mind. A boy who grew up angry at the world, with only two dishonest men as guides. Of the young man trying to fill his emptiness with drink. She thought off Jack, the very embodiment of evil; a man with no conscience who chose to destroy the life of his own son.

Finally, she got out of the chair and went to where Awk lay. "Awk," she said softly. "You did not destroy my life. You caused me a lot of heartache and pain. I was a victim of your cruelty, yes, but eventually I realized what you did to me was the culmination of your own problems. I would do my best at picking up the pieces of my own life without the extra burden of self-pity. My life would have been destroyed if I had not let go of the rage and hatred that I felt towards you and my own father. Instead of brooding over it, I have gone on with whatever I had to do to survive. If that is forgiveness you are already forgiven. As far as leaving nothing for me, I can make it on my own. Don't worry about that now."

She helped him back to his bed and placed a cool cloth on his fevered forehead. As he looked up at her she had another glimpse of the hurting little boy who just wanted a place to belong. *Love is a strange emotion,* she thought. She could never love Awk like she had loved Johnny, but she felt a different kind of love toward Awk. It was a mix of compassion, forgiveness and a deep caring for this man who was broken and injured by what life had handed him. She bent and placed a kiss on his burning cheek. "Goodnight my husband," she said softly. "I hope the pain lets you sleep."

She phoned Eileen that night. There was the usual small talk as they discussed the recent trip the couple had taken, then after a pause she said, "Awk is very ill. They brought him here to die. Can you come soon? He needs to be able to say, "Goodbye," to his Mom before he dies."

"So he told you?" Eileen's voice was husky with emotion. "I will be there as soon as I can get ready."

She arrived early the next morning, her face stressed and drawn as if she had not slept. The two women embraced, weeping together. "You must think I am a terrible person not to have been there when my son was a baby," Eileen sobbed. "That is why I was so insistent that you love Little Robby when he was born. I couldn't tell you then that he was my Grandson, and I always felt that it was my fault that Awk became the person he did. He never had a mother. My father never even let me see him when he was born. He took me far away and told me not to come back until I was married and had children. The only reason I ever came back was that I wanted to be with my son, but by then it was too late. The damage was done."

"You were still a little girl scared of your father. I understand fully." She led the older woman to the bedside of her son and quietly left the room. This was their time together, not only to say, "Goodbye," but to heal the broken bonds of a mother and her first born son. Eileen would stay until he passed, sharing what little time was left with this broken child of hers.

Three days later he breathed his last as his mother cradled him in her arms, and Rawhide held his hand. He had a peaceful smile on his face, knowing at last, a small part of what it was like to have people love him and care about him.

There was no funeral service for Awk at his own request. Just a lonely burial with Eileen and Rawhide weeping by the grave as his coffin was lowered. His life was over and they both grieved, not for his passing but for a little boy who never felt loved and wanted.

That evening Rawhide stepped out on the veranda. She heard the nighthawks in their endless chase of insects, saw the fireflies in the taller grass by the trees, listened to birds chirp sleepily in the trees. This would be her last night in this big house. Had it only been less than four years? It seemed like a lifetime ago when all this began. She felt a chill of apprehension. What lay ahead for her? After all her talk of forgiveness she knew she could never forgive Jack for his cruelty. Rawhide hoped he was out of their lives forever. She and Eileen had agreed that no one was to be told that Jack was Robby's grandfather. They were the only two living people that knew and it must stay that way to protect Robby from ever finding out

****

Far away on that very day a tired older woman was trudging through a cabbage field, gathering cabbages. For her there was no future. She was alone, without a family. Heavy work claimed her futile existence.

CHAPTER 20

Rawhide and the little boys were soon settled in their new home. There was a happy reunion with her parents and the joyful first meeting of her Grandfather Burak. She shyly gave her father a hug, the same hug she used to give him when life was happy. That hug told him he was forgiven, and he wrapped his arms around her and cried.

Nataliya had prepared a wonderful meal. Rawhide had forgotten what a good cook her mother was and momentarily envied the hospital patients who got to eat her food every day. There was a greater treat coming! As soon as the meal was cleared away, Nataliya helped Peter to his feet. They sang together. Happy memories of her childhood came rushing back as she wriggled between her parents, and put her arms around both their waists and joined in. For a moment it felt like she was their little girl again. Grandpa Burak soon joined in the singing. Before long Robby and Alexander were adding their little voices.

This was "family" and she rejoiced in the healing, yet even as she rejoiced, thoughts of the damage Jack's dishonesty had caused her family and how he had hurt his own son, Awk, overwhelmed her. Her family was battered and would heal but for Awk there would be no true healing, no further chance. He was gone. Tears were running down her cheeks by the time the song ended, and everyone was looking at her. She said nothing. How would they understand her grieving for someone who had hurt her so badly, someone she did not even miss? It was not grief for herself but for Awk who had been treated so cruelly as a child and never knew love or how to love.

The following day Rawhide had taken the little boys up for Grandma Eileen to babysit while she looked for work. She was about to leave when Frank called her and asked her to wait a minute because they wanted to talk to her.

"We know how well you did on completing your high school on your own," he began. "We know how often you have said you wished you could study law. "Things have been financially tight for us during and since the depression. Eileen has a heart of pure gold and let the farmers stay on their land even when they could not even pay their taxes. She personally carried that load for years, paying taxes so that no one would lose their land and whatever equity they had in it. Presently, she is working with the farmers and hoping they will agree for the banks take over the loans if, and when that is possible. There is a lot of work to be done and a lot of legal hoops to jump through and it is going to take time." Believe me, it will be a relief for us when we no longer have all the financial headaches of providing financing for the farmers!

"Things have been pretty tight for us since we purchased this house," he continued, "but some of the farmers have been able to begin paying us again. We talked it over and we have enough income to make you an offer. We will take care of the little boys while you attend University classes every day. We will pay for your first year and see if this is really what you want to do. We won't charge you rent, but we will ask you to do things like wash windows and mow the lawn.

She could not believe her ears. It was a dream come true, but it was so much for them to do for her. They had done so much for her already with helping her on the farm and providing her with a home and child care. Now they were offering her a chance to pursue her dream, even when they were having some financial struggles of their own.

"Are you sure?" she stammered, then quickly added, "Yes, I really want to go to University if you mean it." Within moments she was jumping up and down and squealing for joy!

"Then get yourself down there and enroll because there are not many days before classes begin!" Frank chuckled.

Once in the Registrar's office, things did not move as smoothly as she had imagined. She had never thought that girls did not study law and she might not be accepted. There had to be a board meeting to see if she could enroll. She waited days for that decision and was delighted when it was decided to accept her application on the strength of her perfect High School marks, although she was warned:

"She must not be a distraction to the men in her classes or she would be dismissed."

Rawhide rushed home with the good news that she had been accepted, almost crushing Eileen and Frank in her excited hugs!

Life settled in to a routine. Nataliya was happy to be able to spend time with her son Alexander, at last, and took him to be with her when she was not working at the hospital. This gave Eileen a much-needed break. Before long Robby wanted to spend time with his other Grandma as well. It did cause the little boys some confusion. They could both call Eileen, "Grandma," but Alexander called Nataliya "Mom," while Robby was to call her "Grandma." There was no end of arguments between the boys until they finally accepted this division of Grandma and Mom titles.

Rawhide found attending Law School had some similarities to her first day of school in the little country school she had attended, as far as acceptance went. She was a woman in a man's world where she was not welcomed. She was met with whistles, rude gestures, pokes in her back and opinions about where women belonged. She had no choice except to ignore them and carry on with her studies. There was no friend like Johnny here to put them in their place, she was on her own. It was not long before she was head of her class, which only increased the verbal abuse directed at her.

Stressful as it was for her, Rawhide finished that year with the highest honors and was eager to continue. Frank and Eileen happily agreed to pay for another year, proud of her accomplishment.

Nataliya had heard of an opening in the hospital kitchen and put in a good word for Rawhide to work there through the summer so she could add to the saving fund for Alexander's operation. Everyone was saving all they could, but the operation would be costly, and the fund was still small. Frank and Eileen were adding to it as well during the summer when they were not paying for Rawhides tuition.

CHAPTER 21

Now that World War Two was over, Natalia and her father, Ivan Burak had one goal and that was to find Olena and Anicha if they were still living. How they were going to do that, they did not know. If they could have gone to the Ukraine and been able to come home again it might have been easier, but they did not dare risk it.

Ivan was finally was able to locate the address of an old friend to see if he had any idea if Olena and Anicha were alive and where they might be if they were. The friend gave him little reassurance after he searched through directories with no record of them anywhere in Ukraine. So many people had died in the villages and and cities, including Kiev, that there were no records of all the dead.

This man had another friend that used a different angle and asked Ivan if he remembered names of any of her friends or relatives that she might have gone to during the famine. Ivan supplied all the names he could remember and waited, hoping for some clue. A clue finally came. Olena had arrived in Kiev to stay in the home of a distant relative. Although not a wealthy man he was able to provide food for her, at least for a time. Anicha soon became a maid in the home of a doctor. She had always wanted to be a doctor herself, so it wasn't long before she was helping the doctor as an assistant. From what this friend could find out this kindly doctor had some connections in the United States. Before the war broke out the doctor was able to get Anicha to the US to study medicine, all expenses paid. Her benefactor was now deceased. She had gone alone without Olena. No one had any idea where she was now or what had become of Olena. Much of Kiev was destroyed shortly after as the Nazis took control of Ukraine. There was no record of Olena after that time.

Nataliya searched for endless months trying to locate a Dr. Anicha Burak connected to hospitals in the US. She had little to go on and finally gave up trying. Although she grieved for her mother and tried not to think of all she must have gone through, she rejoiced that her sister was safe and probably alive and well.

****

Nataliya had just taken a large bowl of salad to the cafeteria one day when she saw a woman waiting in line for food. *Could this be Anicha?* she wondered, trying not to stare. She had not seen her sister for almost twenty years, but she thought she saw some resemblance to her little sister. Finally, getting the courage, she walked up to where she could speak to her. "Are you new here," she asked. "I haven't seen you down here before."

Instead of an answer the woman exclaimed, "Nataliya is this you?" and clapped her hands. They flew into each other's arms, not caring anything about the looks and stares they were receiving. They only had moments as Nataliya was at work, but she gave her their father's address. Anicha promised she would come that evening.

The evening meal was a festive event. Rawhide joined them, anxious to meet this aunt that she could not remember at all. Her aunt was Dr. Anicha now, although she called herself Dr. Anne. She introduced the tall man beside her as "Dr. Dan."

Ivan Burak was almost overwhelmed as he hugged his youngest daughter to himself. He kept sobbing,"My baby, my little baby. I never thought I would hold my baby girl again! I just can't believe this is you!"

The rest of the family fired question after question at Anicha regarding her life and what she might know about where Olena was. Anicha became their link to some of what had happened in the Old Country as they called it.

The family waited impatiently after Anicha told them all to be quiet and listen, and she would tell them everything she knew.

After graduating, Anicha had a dream of coming to Canada to see if she could locate her sister and Katjia. Since her husband and fellow doctor was a Canadian, it was easy for them both to find work in Canada. Finding her sister was the hard part. She had written letters to the address she had for Nataliya and Peter, but they all came back, RETURN TO SENDER. ADDRESS UNKNOWN.

The couple were on vacation now and hoped that by using the address they had for Nataliya, they would be able to locate her. Of course, they found the town, but no one seemed to know where Nataliya Romanov was. One of Anicha's fellow classmates was a doctor at this hospital, and they had made a date to have lunch together in the cafeteria, and visit while they dined. It was only by the rarest chance that she and Nataliya had met there!

The big question left to answer was, "Where is Olena?"

"I don't know," she answered sadly. "She was staying with this family when I left, and I had hoped that as soon as I had a place to live for myself, she could come and join me. By the time I did, she was no longer there. I do not know if you have heard these things out here, or not, but over three million Ukrainian peasants were purposely starved to death under Stalinist rules between 1932 and 1933.

Fortunately, we had left the village before the country side was sealed off by the soldiers. After it was sealed off, no one could go anywhere to escape the famine, but even then, it was a hard time for our mother. The relative she was staying with was old and I am not sure he had much food either at times. The doctor I worked for was very kind, and I often was able to take baskets of food to our mother which helped her some. I left in 1936. I never heard from her again after I left. I try not to think of all of us having at least enough food and our poor mother, who did so much for us, was left there on her own. The Nazis took over and there was much bloodshed. I don't know anything more."

Ivan looked thoughtful. "I wonder if it would be safe for me to go to Ukraine and search for her?"

Dr. Anne shook her head, "No, my father. Right now, there is still a lot of unrest and a different Soviet Government. We don't want to lose you. There has to be a better way. I am going back to Toronto tomorrow, but we will keep in touch and do all we can to find our poor mother."

****

The old woman shuffled slowly toward the stable to milk the cow, her swollen legs making each step she took a major effort. She wondered how life had forced her to finally do this lowly task of milking cows in order to earn a place to sleep and a little bread. She felt like every bite of food she ate was begrudged her unless she worked very hard to earn it. Life was hard. She had been taken to Germany and forced into a Nazi slave labor camp with many others. She was among the few survivors. She had worked on a farm and the aging German couple who owned it took pity on her and would often give her bread when no one was looking.

When the Nazis lost the war, most of the surviving laborers were sent to the Soviet gulags and numbers of them died there. She had been taken in by the old couple as their hired help instead of her being sent to the gulags. It was only because of them that she still lived, and she was grateful to them in spite of how hard she had to work on their farm. She was a survivor, but a survivor without a future or a family. She knew she would likely die alone in Germany, so far away from her loved ones.

She had a daughter who had left Ukraine and moved to Canada. Her other daughter had gone to the US. Each had promised to have her join them, but they had not done so before the famine or the war. She felt they had forgotten her. Now, after all these years, she did not even know where they were and certainly, they would not know where she was. Lonely tears slid down her leathery face, thinking of her family and hoping all was well with them. "Maybe I will try one more time to write to my daughter in Canada as soon as this cow is milked," she decided as she seated herself heavily on the stool beside the cow.

She wrote the letter without any hope of an answer. Once the letter was written she shuffled wearily to the village to mail it, wondering why she was still so foolish to even hope.

She took a chance and the chance bore fruit. Rawhide's friend, Charlene, had gone back to the farm to visit her parents and had stopped at the Post Office to see another friend, Amy, who worked there. They shared some memories and then Amy suddenly asked, "Do you have any idea where Nataliya Romanov is? This letter with some funny words on it came a few weeks ago for her. I don't have a forwarding address and I can't figure out how to send it back to wherever it came from."

Charlene picked up the letter. I don't have an address, but I see Rawhide quite often. I will give it to her for her mother.

****

When Nataliya gave the letter to her father, he sat and cried, his hands trembling. "She is alive, my Olena is still alive," he sobbed. "How can I get her here?"

He wrote a letter back and posted it the next morning along with a letter from Nataliya. Anne was called, and she began working through all the hurdles of getting her mother to Canada. It would be expensive, and it was not a quick process, but it looked like it could be done. In faraway Germany, Olena cried with joy. Her Ivan was still alive! Her girls were safe! The long, painfilled years of wandering were almost over, and if all went well, they would all be together once more.

****

Rawhide was in her third year of studies. The male students had slowly accepted her being there and life became less stressful. She had many lively debates with a fellow student named Jason. She remained the honor student, but he was not far behind. Slowly the debates took on a friendlier nature. They occasionally went out for dinners, so they could talk and get to know each other better. They enjoyed these times together. It was clear he was infatuated with her, but for Rawhide there was a feeling of reserve. Was it because he was so unlike Johnny or was it something else about him? He was handsome, self-assured and certainly diligent about his goal of becoming a lawyer. All good qualities, but she felt a distance growing on her part.

It was one of those dinner dates when out of the blue he asked, "Why do women waste their time getting an education? Are they showing off how smart they are to the guys, or just what is their goal?" Her response was quick. "So, you are referring to me then? I don't see anyone else in our classes for you to be singling out."

"Hey! Don't get all your feathers ruffled," he grinned. "I was just referring to women in general. When I get married, I do want to marry an educated woman, so I know she is smart enough for me, but I will never let her work out of the home. She will be 'Queen of my Castle,' and nothing else."

"Well, that shines a light on who you are. An educated girl might not want to marry you. Your mother runs a business so where does that put her in your opinion?"

He squirmed uncomfortably. This conversation was headed in a direction he had never planned. "It is different with my mother. She inherited a lot of money to start her business. She never wasted time chasing a big education and she didn't work either. She hired people to do it for her and she hasn't done much except sit back and enjoy the profits of her venture."

"In that case my friend, why are you wasting your time dating a penniless peasant, as one of our esteemed classmates has recently referred to me as being." She smiled as she rose from the table. "This peasant has children to support and she needs an education to do that. Right now, she needs to get home and put those aforementioned children to bed, so if you would kindly drive me home, I would appreciate it."

He apologized over and over on the way home, telling her how much he loved her and what he had been getting at was that he would love and care for a wife and she would never need to work.

She only smiled and thanked him for dinner as she left the car.

He asked her out several times more, appearing eager to understand her viewpoint and trying to make it clear that if they were married, he would respect her decision to work. It seemed like it was bringing them closer, yet those doubts still niggled in the back of her mind. There was something about him that made her feel uneasy about taking their friendship further, yet she was not sure what it was.

Their friendship remained static until her final year. She was caught up in the needs of her little boys and her parents. Any thoughts of Jason were pushed to the back of her mind.

The big excitement in the family was that as soon as enough money was raised, dear Grandmother Olena would be able to come to Canada, and be reunited with her husband, and the rest of the family. The problem was that everyone was putting every spare penny they had, into the fund for Alexander's surgery

Even Anicha and Dan who were heavily in debt from purchasing a home and setting up their clinic as well as paying off the balance of Dan's medical school bill, were adding their bit to Alexanders surgery fund.

Little Alexander insisted they use that to bring his Grandma to Canada. The family had a meeting that Eileen and Frank were invited to. It was a difficult situation. Alexander needed surgery but it looked like it would still be a long time until there would be enough money for this. There was not enough to bring Olena over either, but it would be possible within a few more months

Eileen spoke up. "This is only my opinion, but since Olena is not well, I do not believe she will be able to remain where she is for very long. She needs to be with her family, and she needs medical help as well. Alexander is not in critical condition at this time. His quality of life will be much better once he has that surgery, but he does not have to have it immediately. Two of the farms I am financing have made the decision to refinance through the bank and I will be paid out. This will happen by next year. I will loan the money to pay for Alexander's operation then, if the family will accept this."

It was a difficult decision, but the family finally agreed with Alexander to name the fund the 'Grandmother Fund.' In a few more months there would be enough money raised, to bring Olena to join her family

CHAPTER 22

Robby had started school. Rawhide was thrilled to find out he had championed the cause of another child who was being bullied … like his Uncle Johnny before him had done! She was so proud of her boy. It may not have seemed a big thing to others, but she knew that act of kindness could change the boy's own life and ripple down to his descendants.

Alexander did not have the strength to go to school, yet she did not want him to get behind. He was a bright little boy and when that miracle of an operation could happen, as it would soon, both Nataliya and Rawhide wanted him to be able to fit right into his age group at school.

Eileen had promised to loan the money for Alexander's surgery as soon as she could. Until then he needed schooling. Eileen, ever caring for the needs of others, offered to teach him at home and he was enrolled in the Correspondence School.

Meanwhile, Jason was persistent. Even though Rawhide was still friendly toward him, he could sense Rawhide becoming more distant. Whenever he would ask for a date she was "too busy." He was unsure how to win her heart, but he was a determined man, used to getting his own way.

His Mother was hosting a gala dinner event for all the "rich and important" in her circle. She called them "High Society". This would be a golden opportunity to introduce her to what his life was like and have her meet his mother. Maybe then she would understand all the advantages he could offer, compared to her working for a living.

To her own surprise she agreed to go with him to the event.

"I am going to buy you the perfect dress to wear to the gala," he insisted.

"Why would you do that? I buy my own clothes and I don't want somebody else deciding what I should wear." Her voice sounded irritated.

"I just want you to wear something, er, special. Like a gift from me." He was thankful he had stopped before he said the word, "appropriate." It was what he meant though. He knew his mother would be scrutinizing his date from the moment she set eyes on the girl. Therefore, he wanted nothing but perfection in her attire for that evening. It had to be expensive or it wouldn't pass! Rawhide always wore skirts and sweaters to class, she probably had nothing else. Showing up at this dinner, dressed like that, would be a disaster!

Rawhide said nothing. He took her silence as acceptance, so he went about selecting a dress he could feel proud of her wearing in his company. He knew what her tastes were, so he searched until he found a dress that was both modest and would accent her natural beauty. And now, matching shoes, of course! He could not risk her coming to the gala in the brown loafers she always wore to class!

The dress was beautiful. The creamy peach colored silk creation was simply styled. It was sleeveless and featured a high neck neckline. The wide, A-line skirt draped gracefully to her ankles.

She slipped the dress over her head, reveling in the liquid sensation of the silk surrounding her body. As she put on the matching shoes, she wondered if this was what he meant by his wife being the "Queen of His Castle." It would be a life foreign to everything she had ever known. Was she independent simply because she had never known anything but having to struggle to survive? A life of ease and luxury was within her reach, only waiting for her to accept. Maybe she was missing out on an easier life. She was weakening. If he asked her again, tonight, she knew she would say "yes."

Jason gasped when he saw her. The color and cut of the dress perfectly accented her cascade of black curls and her soft tan skin. "I knew you were beautiful, but in this dress. Wow! You are going to overwhelm the crowd ... especially my mother!" Helping her into the car he apologized. "Sorry, but we are running late and it's not a good thing to keep my Mama waiting. Keep your eyes shut because we are taking a short cut through a section of the city you won't want to see."

She kept her eyes wide open. She remembered those streets well Streets with poorly dressed people walking aimlessly down the sidewalks, looks of desperation on their faces. She saw a young girl on the street corner and knew with a shudder that she was living a life that could have been hers. What was that poor girl's story that brought her here to this? Rawhide forgot the princess dress she was wearing, as a burning desire to be a voice for the poor, filled her mind. At that moment she knew she would never be the queen of anyone's castle unless the keeper of the castle could understand this need in her. It would be impossible for her to live a life of ease when there were hurting people she could help. She knew without any doubt that Jason could not understand that need.

Jason was unaware of her changed mood and her silence. He bounced her into the huge dining room of his mother's mansion and loudly introduced her as, "Kathy Belker, the girl of my dreams," before seating her between his mother and himself. As he sat down, he flashed his charming smile to the other guests.

She seethed. Her legal name was Katjia. She knew instantly why he had called her Kathy. Katjia was a Ukrainian name and to say it would immediately connect her to the hard working, but poor immigrants who came to Canada looking for freedom. Jason would not use it because he knew his mother, and probably most of her friends, would not accept her if he used her name. The almost forgotten memory of being called "Bohunk," echoed through her mind. This was a polite way of saying exactly the same insulting thing. Being half Russian would only make it worse since "Russian" and "Communist" were often used in the same breath. She clenched her fists under the table and smiled what she hoped was a polite smile.

The older lady looked her over as if she was choosing a live animal to skin for pelts to make one of the exquisite furs her company manufactured. Rawhide got the feeling from the woman's facial expression that if she were an animal, her pelt would be substandard and tossed in the discard pile. After some moments of examination, the lady coolly extended a well-manicured hand. It was not a real handshake but only a brushing of hands.

Everyone sat in silence for several strained minutes until Jason's mother addressed the younger woman. "So what line of business is your father in, Kathy?" she asked.

Rawhide thought quickly. "Unfortunately, my father is an invalid now, but at one time he was a musician."

The older woman snorted. "Not much money in the life of a musician, is there? I suppose he never had the gumption to get a decent paying job instead. We have streets here in the city filled with people like him. Always whining about being poor but never getting out there and getting a decent job to look after their families."

By now Rawhide's clenched fists were getting sweaty with tension. This was going badly. She had already been outed as a poor girl, so she may as well speak her mind. With the innocence that was her style, she asked, "How can they get a job if no one hires a poor person? Unless there is equal opportunity, they will only be hired out of desperation when an employer has no one else to choose from."

She could feel the eyes of the older lady glaring at her as she went on. "You have a high-end clothing store that sells only top-quality garments. Just suppose you have a job opening. Two young girls apply with equal credentials, such as good grades and good character ratings. You decide to interview both these young women. They are both attractive, intelligent girls. One comes to the interview well dressed and her hair done in a fashionable style. The other comes dressed almost in rags, her hair neat and clean but tied back with a band. Which one are you going to hire?"

"The one that took her time to get ready for the interview," snapped the lady. "The other one shows she is just trash and I can tell you a business like mine doesn't hire trash. I send this kind of trash to a Madam who can use anyone. That is where girls like this belong."

Rawhide sucked in her breath. The old lady was getting angry, but so was she. This was hitting very close to her own past. "The girl you didn't hire was probably wearing the only dress she owned. She had no money to get her hair styled or buy a fashionable dress for the interview. You hired the other one on looks only and sent the poor girl to the streets. This is not equal opportunity. This is why the streets are filled, as you say, with whining, hungry people. For a thousand different reasons they have been knocked down and without a kind hand to reach down and give them equal opportunity, they have no way of getting that 'good job' you say they should get."

By now the older lady was furious. "Jason," she shrieked. "I don't know where you found this peasant woman but get her out of here! Now! I don't want scum like her eating at my table!"

Jason hurried Rawhide out of the room. "Whatever got in to you to talk to my mother like that," he hissed. "Keep your own warped ideas about the condition of the poor to yourself." Glaring at her, he shouted, "And as for you and me, it's over!"

Rawhide smiled. "Thank you for saying that, Jason. It saves me telling you the very same thing."

He pulled up to her door. "Hand that dress and those shoes out to me. I won't have a person like you wearing anything like that. You showed up as trash to my mother and trash doesn't wear clothes like that!"

She stifled the urge to roll the dress in a ball and throw it out the door at him, followed by the shoes. Instead, she placed them neatly in the boxes and gave them to him.

Just as she was coming back from taking the boxes to Jason, Eileen came down the stairs. "I take it you came home from the party a bit early." She looked quizzically at Rawhide.

Rawhide smiled a little. "Let's just say I found out why I don't want to be married to Jason and be called Kathy for the rest of my life. Can you imagine me going through life, not daring to think my own thoughts or have an opinion of my own? His mother called me a peasant among other things. I just realized I was born a peasant, raised a peasant and for the rest of my life my heart will be the heart of a peasant. That's just who I am, that is where I belong, and nothing will change that. Most of my work will be with poor people who are being squished down every time they try to stand up. These are people who can't afford a lawyer to speak for them. I will be that voice." Her face wore a look of determination as she spoke.

Eileen hugged the girl as she said, "Rawhide. Johnny's tough little Rawhide! He would be so proud of you right now if he were here. I am his Mom, and I am proud of you too. "

CHAPTER 23

The following morning Jason and Rawhide avoided each other as much as it was possible to do since they were in the same classes. To make it even more complicated, this was the day they were to conduct a mock trial in front of the other budding young lawyers. She was designated the lawyer for the "victim."

There was no reason for this to be in the local paper except that Jason's mother wanted the publicity for her son. He would be looking for a position in a law office soon. This bit of publicity would ensure him an immediate position since she was sure her son would "win his case" and future employers would be impressed.

There was publicity, but not the publicity she hoped for. Her son lost to the fast thinking Rawhide, who left him stammering for words. The reporter interviewed each of them later. The interviews were in the morning paper the next day.

Reporter: "Jason Wilbur Smythe. You lost in this mock trial. In real life you will lose from time to time. What knowledge have you gained from this experience that will prepare you for real trials?"

Jason: "I would have to examine the evidence more critically than I did on this occasion."

Reporter: "What are your future goals in the field of law?"

Jason: "My plan is to do an excellent job for clients who are well able to pay for my services. I do not plan to do any Pro Bono services as this would greatly lower my standards and my reputation."

The reporter turned to Rawhide:

"Mrs. Belker: I see here that your given name is Katjia, but I have heard you referred to as Rawhide by your classmates on several different occasions. Why this moniker?"

Rawhide: "What does rawhide make you think of?"

Reporter: "Something that even my dog can't chew."

Rawhide: Smiled.

Reporter: "So you won this mock trial. What do you attribute this to?"

Rawhide: "I looked for hidden clues and followed those leads. In this way I took my opponent by surprise."

Reporter: "What are your future goals as a lawyer?"

Rawhide: "My main purpose will be to give poor people a voice when they have been taken advantage of."

The next morning Jason and his mother gathered all the newspapers they could find and burned them. "How could you ever let that peasant woman take advantage of you like that? What kind of names are these? Katjia? Rawhide? This girl has no class at all," she shouted at Jason. "I don't know why you were ever attracted to a woman like that! I thought you had better taste! They should never have let her study law in the first place, she is just trash! This is such a disgrace and we will never live this down."

Jason was silent, his face red.

****

Two days later one of the Professors called Rawhide out of class. "You have been requested to go to the Legal Office of Smith and Sons immediately. All your classes will be excused for the day." She left with a rodent of fear gnawing in her stomach

The lawyer smiled as he offered her a seat. "Well Katjia Belker, better known as Rawhide, we meet again under more favorable circumstances than a few years ago. I am sincerely glad to see that. Kids in trouble break my heart." She let out a sigh of relief as he went on. "We have had a hard time locating you, but that newspaper article helped us in our search. I have some good news for you. But I think you need to be sitting in that chair since plucking people off the floor is not my specialty." He smiled as he picked up an envelope of papers.

Her eyes wide, Rawhide accepted the chair.

"Well, Mrs. Belker," the Lawyer continued. "It seems you were once engaged to a lad named Johnny Carpenter who had some valuable property. He went to war but before he left, he willed everything to you, his fiancé, in case anything happened to him. On Dec 8, 1941 Johnny was reported missing in action somewhere in the South Pacific during the Battle of Pearl Harbor. The required wait time is over, and we have spent more time attempting to locate you. We tried to contact his parents, but they evidently have either moved or deceased as the Post Office did not forward our letter. That article in the newspaper about the debate helped, as there was reference to you being referred to as 'Rawhide'. It didn't take much more to find that Rawhide Romanov and Rawhide Belker were the same lady and we had a place to contact you.

He smiled at her shocked face. "I am handing you the deed and title to Johnny's land after we do some signing. There is more though. Johnny had mineral rights on this land. Numerous producing oil wells are on that land and have been for years. You are getting more than his land. There is a great deal of money in a trust account in your name."

When the papers were signed, and a bank account opened in her name, the lawyer helped the shaking girl to the door. "By the way, Mrs. Belker, as soon as you pass your bar exams there will be a position waiting for you in our firm. Good day now."

She caught the bus to go home, hoping she had the presence of mind to have thanked the lawyer.

She went quietly to her suite, hoping Eileen would not hear her. Going to her dresser, she took out the packet of letters from Johnny and re-read them all. His words in the last letter took on a deeper meaning. "No matter what happens to you, no matter what happens to me, I will always take care of you, Little Rawhide. Be strong."

Johnny! He had always been there for her from that awful first day of school. He believed in her, encouraged her and made her feel part of a larger group. Yes, he was still taking care of her with this huge gift, but he had given her a greater gift of self-esteem a long time ago. She hugged his letters to her heart and cried herself to sleep. Eileen found her there, tears dried on her face and a bundle of letters scattered around her. On the floor lay the title to Johnny's land. She woke her gently. "Do you want to tell me now or later?"

Rawhide sat up and hugged the older woman. "Your son willed me all his land along with a lot of oil revenue. I don't even know what to say or do. This sounds crazy, but I don't want money. I just want Johnny home."

Eileen remained standing, too shocked to sit down. Frank soon joined them. This was their own son who had done this for the brave little girl he loved, but it all seemed impossible and unreal. Rawhide finally spoke. "Thanks so much for believing in me and paying my way through legal school. Your son, who also believed in me, will be paying you back soon. I will do my best to be the person you all believed in!"

Frank and Eileen circled her in a group hug. They spent the evening sitting in her suite together, trying to let the reality of Johnny's gift sink in while dining on crackers and soup, which was all she had in her apartment to eat.

Word spread quickly. All her classmates had heard the news before she arrived in first class. When she came to the door the others were standing and she entered the room to a chorus of cheers and clapping. Everybody wanted to talk about it. She didn't. Tears were too close to the surface. She missed Johnny more than ever. Did they think money meant that much to her? She would live in poverty forever if she could just have Johnny here instead of his money!

Jason more or less followed her around until he finally found a moment to talk to her alone. "My mother wanted you to know she has thought over what you said to her the other night, and it is OK. She will never hold that against you. She hopes you and I get back together. So how about dinner tonight to celebrate your big windfall? I can help you plan ways to invest your money wisely. Mother has some ideas about good investments for ladies to make as well. She is even considering asking you to partner with her in her clothing business."

She looked at him coolly. "Jason, I like you or at least I thought I did for a while, but there was always something missing. Something never quite seemed to click for me. Yesterday, I finally realized what it was. You have a plan of who I can be, what I can think, and what I can do with my life. You obviously still do, but you are not considering the plans I have made for my own life."

She stopped for a moment. "Just a few days ago, you and your mother called me 'peasant trash' and wanted nothing more to do with me. Almost overnight I become a multi-millionaire and you are pretending the insults never happened, not because you love me, but because you love money. You are now expecting me to let you decide how to invest my money, how to use my money, and how to live my life. I don't want you to do that, and I don't need you to do that. I have some basic intelligence of my own. I know what I am going to do without any help from you or your sweet Mommy."

She looked right in his eyes as she spoke. "There is a big difference between you and Johnny. He loved me for who I was, and he let me be free to be myself. He loved me when I was the ragged little kid they called 'Baby Bohunk' and 'Cattle Thief.' I had no shoes except some chunks of rawhide that my father shaped into boots and they called me Rawhide because of this. Johnny accepted and loved me just the way I was and never expected to change me into something I wasn't. To put it in simple language, Jason, I could never fit in your mold. You need to go find a little puppet that can enjoy being a prisoner in your castle. It will never be me!"

****

A few weeks later her family sat in the waiting room of the hospital, where Alexander was having high risk surgery. For Nataliya, the thought she might lose him was unbearable and almost made her cancel the operation. She had lost two sons at birth and her heart was breaking at the thought of losing Alexander. Sick as he was, he was still her pride and joy. Of course, she wanted him to be well and strong, but the risk was almost too great for her to give permission for something this serious.

It was the boy himself that talked her into signing the papers. "Mother," he said. "I want this chance to be strong and healthy. It is no fun just sitting here watching Robby doing fun things that I can't do. Please give me that chance. Do what you have to do, Mother and let's get this over with."

With trembling hands, she signed the consent form, agreeing to trust her child's life into the hands of the surgeon.

Hours dragged by. Rawhide sat by her mother, encouraging her, talking hope and wiping her mother's tears. They all talked about Alex, the funny things he said, how he was fascinated by engineering, how he had learned to play the father's violin without lessons … .Yes, Alex was a special gift to the family.

"It's done," the surgeon announced as he walked through the door, "It was a tough go, but the little guy is a real fighter. He is going to be out there playing baseball in a few weeks."

Once the boy was brought home he was pampered and waited on until he shouted, "Stop it you guys! I have been a baby all my life. Now I am going to be a tough guy and do it all on my own!"

****

Rawhide had surprised her Grandfather Burak by giving him the rest of the money he needed to finally bring his wife to Canada. It was an exciting time for all. With Alexander's surgery safely in the past, Natalia could hardly wait to see her mother. Deciding that her parents needed to have their home to themselves she began a search for a place for Alexander, Peter and herself. She finally found a one-story bungalow that suited their needs.

Stairs worried her. Peter could not climb them safely and she feared he might fall someday while she was at work. This house was perfect. No stairs meant less worries. Rawhide gave Nataliya the money for the down payment and would have happily purchased the house, but her mother insisted on making the rest of the house payments herself. At Rawhide's insistence, Peter had finally agreed to let Nataliya book an appointment to see a specialist. Hopefully there would be help for his ever-worsening condition.

****

Olena flew to Toronto where Anicha met her exhausted, ill, and shabbily dressed mother. After a week of getting Olena the medical help she needed, a good rest and shopping for a new wardrobe, they flew together to join the others. Everyone went to the airport but stayed back to give Ivan and Olena a chance to meet alone. The two aging ones rushed into each other's arms, laughing, sobbing and shouting each other's names. For over thirty years, against impossible odds, they had held on to the hope of someday being together again. Now, they did not waste time mourning the lost years, but rejoiced in the present miracle of being together at last.

Olena was no longer strong. The years of hunger and work in the Nazi slave labor camp had taken a toll on her health. The family all rallied around her, filling her with vitamins and good food until she pushed them away. "I think you are going to kill me with kindness," she would laugh. "Just love me and let me rest a while! I will be alright soon. My road in life has been very long and rough, but it looks smooth now, so I plan to travel on for a while longer. Don't worry so much!"

Alexander was feeling well again so Rawhide and Grandpa Burak loaded all the family into their cars and drove back to the old homestead. Brush had grown up, but the dugout home and the barn were still standing strong. Once inside the little home Olena got a small glimpse of the life her once daring and fearless Nataliya had lived. She understood why her daughter had never sent for her as she had promised to. She was proud of the strength of her daughter to survive during those hard years.

She looked over at the beautiful Katjia, the little granddaughter that she had once said held the hope of the family future in her hands. Young as she was, the girl had struggled through her own hardship. Like herself they were all strong women who never gave up but faced life head on, doing what they had to do to survive. To finally have the family together again was nothing short of a miracle. Anicha, her quiet daughter had enjoyed an easier life compared to the others in the family, yet it had not been easy to be alone in a strange country, studying hard to get her medical degree, while wondering if her family were safe. She too, was strong, in her own way. The kindness she always showed to the elderly in the Ukrainian village was still there, visible in the way she treated her patients and Olena herself.

Rawhide showed Alexander the pole beds and told him this was where he was born. The boy was excited. "Does this mean it is my farm?" he asked eagerly.

"Well, no," she replied. "It has gone back for unpaid taxes and right now nobody owns it."

"Then I will buy it," he said firmly. "It is my farm because I was born here. After Father sees the doctor he can get well again, just like Alexander did and Father and I can be farmers together"

She smiled. He was so full of dreams, this little one. "Maybe there will be help for father, Alexander. We will see if there is anything that can be done for him, but even if he gets well and strong, I don't think he or mother would ever want to live here again."

"Yes, he would, if he has a big strong son like me to help him," Alexander said confidently. I am eight years old already. I could work real hard."

She pinched her little brother's nose and smiled at her mother. "And you thought I was a handful? I was nothing like your son, here!"

CHAPTER 24

The young lawyer was busy with her own private practice. She had worked with the legal firm Smith and Sons for the first year, gaining valuable experience before branching out on her own. She wanted to be able to choose her own clients, as she vowed to only represent the victims. At times identifying the real victims was a challenging task. Quite often the perpetrator of the crime was an excellent liar and came out looking like the victim. She soon realized there were more people like Jack in the world and it challenged her brilliant mind to ferret them out. She had a reputation of being both tough and honest which led to talk among her peers that an honest lawyer was a dangerous enemy in court!

Word reached her that a Native man had been arrested for stealing cattle from a wealthy rancher. *Interesting,* she thought. *I am going to check some things out.* The only name anyone seemed to know for the arrested man was 'Injun Charlie'. *Was this another hate crime intended to cause suffering?"* she wondered. *'Injun Charlie', 'Bohunk Peter'.* "*Those names are racist, and they both were accused of cattle theft. I don't know if Charlie is innocent or not, but if he is, he needs help.*

Racist names are not used in friendly banter. There is masked hatred behind them. When there is hatred there are also false accusations meant to destroy the one who is the victim of racist talk. To Rawhide's keen mind this seemed like it could be a set up to destroy reputations not only for Charlie, but Natives in general.

Her secretary was not in yet, so leaving her a note that she would be out of the office for the day, she found directions and drove to the ranch home of Walter Jenkins, the plaintiff. The ranch house was near the highway. She could see from the highway that the only access to the ranch was a very short driveway to the house yard. A big red barn stood a short distance behind the ranch house. A large white gate, a few feet to the right of the barn, was the sole entry to the pastures beyond. A bunkhouse for the hired hands was built to the right of that white gate. Not a likely place to steal cattle without being seen and heard.

After making a sketch of the layout of the ranch, she drove to the reservation, a distance of forty miles. Her jaunt answered a lot of question in her own mind. Charlie needed help, if he would accept it.

Returning from the reservation she decided to pay a visit to Charlie in the jail. She found him sitting, hunched over and staring at the floor. His face had the same dejected look that she saw in her father's face after Jack had left him a broken man. He too had been accused of a crime he never committed and was voiceless to prove that a crime had been committed against him instead.

Charlie was painfully thin, his rib cage showing through his prison suit. He was a man caught in a system he did not understand and saw no way out. It was his word against a well known and wealthy white man. He could not deny that he had butchered and eaten the steers That meant he had no way to prove he was innocent.

He did not look up when Rawhide entered his cell and spoke. "Hello Mr. Charlie. My name is Katjia Belker. I am a lawyer and I have a feeling I can help you. That's why I am here."

The only response was a grunt. *So what trap is this woman setting for me?* He wondered to himself.

"Look, Mr. Charlie. I do not believe you stole those cattle, but you are going to need a lawyer to fight for you, or they are going to just keep you in prison for a long time without you even having a trial to tell your side of things."

He looked up briefly, desperation registered in his voice as he spoke. "No lawyer is going to help an Indian. I have no money."

"I will help you if you want me to, and I won't charge you anything. If we lose the case, I will pay the court charges myself. You have nothing to lose but, a lot to gain if we win this. I know you are innocent, and I want to prove that as much as you do."

He showed interest, but the wary look of fear had not left his face. He didn't trust her, and she didn't blame him. "Think it over tonight, and I will come by tomorrow morning to see what you have decided," she said as she rose to leave.

"No. Stay now and I will talk. Are you sure you can help me?"

"What I am sure of is that you are an innocent man. I will do my best to convince the judge and jury of that. Nothing is sure, but I am confident you will come out smiling, with your reputation as an honest man restored."

"OK. What do I do?"

"You have to tell me your side of the story, but I am taking you home first. Bail has been set and I will pay it."

They walked out together into the early afternoon sunshine and she led the way to her car. During the ride to the reservation, they only made small talk as she had asked him to wait to tell his side of the story until he could show her any evidence he had. She would need to make sketches of the evidence and take notes as he talked.

His house was a poorly built, very small building, that was covered with tarpaper inside and out. It reminded her of the dirt dugout she had grown up in. He invited her in, and Charlie's wife quickly served her a cup of tea. Rawhide sensed they would have given it to her even if it was all they had left. Sharing and hospitality was their culture. It must make false accusations all the more devastating.

Two hours later she left the cabin with the sketches and Charlie's statements tucked away in her briefcase; more confident than ever he was an innocent man. She could never forget the pain of her family being outcasts in a new country that would not accept her people. It was impossible to fathom what it would be like to be outcasts in your own country with no where to go, one's land and culture gone, and one's children taken. Her heart ached over what she had seen and heard.

She had never wanted to win a trial as much as this one! For one thing, Jason was representing the wealthy rancher. It seemed like a pretty cut and dried case to both of them and they sat smiling. "Caught with the evidence," was good enough! There would be no way out of that! The rancher had smugly made a comment in the Court House hallway that "the only good Injun was a dead Injun."

He and Jason had shared a chuckle as Jason reassured him, "I don't think we can string him up for cattle rustling, but I'll see he gets put away for a good while. This shouldn't even have been brought to trial."

Cows! They were such useful creatures that could provide food, clothing and income but they also be used in the hands of the dishonest to hurt others. Rawhide sighed, realizing that some of her negative experiences in the past had armed her for the battle ahead. Jason had only seen cows in pictures. In fact, as far as she was concerned, he had lived in a bubble all his life and did not know there was life beyond the city.!

Court was soon in session. Mr. Jenkins was sworn in and Jason questioned him, getting the tale that two of his best steers had been stolen. Charlie had been caught red handed with the hides by his house. There wasn't much to this case.

Jason smiled smugly at Rawhide. What a fool she was to bring this to trial when the man was just going to jail anyway when it was over. It was going to feel good to see her make a fool of herself and her client!

It was Rawhides turn to question the rancher. "Mr. Jenkins, there seems to be little doubt that Charlie probably butchered your steers since their hides with your brand on them were found by his house. Is that right?"

"Yes," answered the rancher, barely hiding his smirk.

"Do you know Mr. Charlie?"

"No, I never saw him before today."

"In your opinion, where were your steers butchered?"

"I know they were butchered in his yard. The police saw evidence of that."

"Oh. Did you find the hides there at the same time?"

"Yes. I did"

"A few moments ago, you told Mr. Smythe the RCMP found the hides."

At this point Jason objected, saying she was leading his client. The objection was overruled by the judge.

Rawhide continued. "If the cattle were butchered in Mr. Charlie's yard, how did he get them there?"

"I guess he hauled them there."

"How much did the steers weigh?"

"Oh, maybe about six hundred, eight hundred pounds apiece. At least."

"Since Charlie only has a saddle horse, not a truck, how did he get them to his house?"

"With his horse I guess."

"You told the court your steers weighed six hundred to eight hundred pounds apiece. Is that right?"

"Yes."

"Would you say this thin young man lifted each of those steers on to his horse, and then rode 40 miles down the highway in plain sight, with those two big steers quietly hanging over the horse?"

The courtroom erupted in laughter.

"That's all for now, Mr. Jenkins. You may step down."

She called Charlie next.

"Mr. Charlie, do you know this man?"

"Yes, I do."

"How do you happen to know him?"

"I worked for him, cutting brush this summer."

"Did he pay you?"

"Not with money, but he gave me two steers for my work."

"Oh. Where did you butcher those steers?"

"In my yard like Mr. Jenkins said I did."

"How did the steers get to your yard?"

"Mr. Jenkins hauled them there and helped me butcher them like he said he would."

Jason asked for a recess. He needed to find a way to get out of this and win the case.

Back in court Jason was questioning Mr. Jenkins once more.

"So, you have told me, Mr. Jenkins, that you never saw this person before, but he says he worked for you," he began.

"As I have said, I never saw him before today. He is lying."

"And you did not deliver the steers and help him butcher them, as he has told the court?"

"No! I would never do something like that."

"How do you think he got them to the reservation."

"He probably drove them there. I don't know"

Jason then had a turn questioning Charlie who firmly stuck to his story and could not be led away from it.

Next' it was Rawhides turn.

"I have driven by your ranch, Mr. Jenkins. In order for Mr. Charlie or anyone else to get these cattle to the highway, he would have to drive them past the bunkhouse your ranch hands use, then through your yard and right past your own house. You also have four very large dogs that know how to bark. How do you think he could chase those steers through there without someone knowing it?"

"That would be easy. I was probably asleep."

"And your ranch hands were asleep as well?"

"We work hard. A man needs his sleep."

"I am curious. The assumption is that this stranger rode through your yard, managed to single out these two steers from a stampeding herd, in the dark, then drive them past your bunkhouse and house. They would be bawling, and the dogs barking but you and your men heard nothing?"

"I sleep sound."

"Have you lost a lot of cattle this way, since you, your men and all four dogs sleep this soundly?"

"No these are the only ones I have ever lost."

"Do you know what perjury is, Mr. Jenkins?"

No response.

"I have no further questions. You may step down. May I call Dr. Harrison to the stand please."

"Dr Harrison, do you recognize these two men, Mr. Jenkins and Mr.Charlie?"

"Yes, I do. Mr. Charlie got a bad cut on his leg this summer and Mr. Jenkins brought him to my clinic for stitches. The leg became infected, so they returned several times for treatment."

"Do you know how this injury occurred?"

"Yes, he was cutting brush for Mr. Jenkins and accidently cut his leg with an axe."

"No more questions Dr. Harrison. Mr. Charlie would you show this scar to the court?"

Charlie obediently pulled up his pant leg and showed the jury his scar

"The defense rests, Your Honor."

Jason then addressed the jury with a long-winded speech about the honesty and integrity of his client who was being made to look dishonest. He rambled on at length.

When it was her turn to address the jury, her comments were short. "Members of the jury," she began, "Mr. Charlie was falsely accused of a crime he did not commit, not because he is a dishonest man but because of hatred and racism. You have heard with your own ears and have seen with your own eyes that the plaintiff in this case attempted to set a trap for the defendant. It has been proven that the plaintiff lied under oath. Your decision must be made from the point of honesty. Thank you."

Rawhide seated herself beside Charlie and looked across at Jason. Both he and Jenkins looked concerned.

The jury returned quickly and handed their decision to the Judge. Looking down at Charlie, he said, "You are not guilty, Mr. Charlie. But the jury finds Mr. Jenkins guilty of perjury, defamation of the character of an innocent man and racial discrimination. They also made a recommendation that you should give Mr. Charlie substantial restitution for the stress and misery you have caused him and his family. I have decided to sentence you for your malicious behavior in this way. You will supply Mr. Charlie with meat and flour for his family, for two years, from this date. I am appointing Mrs. Belker to monitor this and report to me monthly, to ensure that this is done. You are also responsible to pay all court costs."

The courtroom erupted in cheers, as one person after another came to shake Charlie's hand.

In the hallway, Jason caught up to Rawhide. "You disgust me. How can you destroy your reputation by taking on the Pro Bono cases of these people anyway?"

Giving him her sweetest smile, she responded, "Thank you for your deep concern about me and my future. I would rather represent an honest poor person than a rich dishonest one. I think you should feel concern for your own reputation if you keep letting these rich boys down like you did today. Maybe you should do some homework next time before you think a case is "simple".

"I hate you, Rawhide. I just want you to know that."

I know, dearest! Aren't you glad you don't have to come home to your gilded Castle and find me there tonight?"

He could not miss her mocking message in that statement. He angrily left to talk to his unhappy client.

She found Charlie and his wife waiting by her car. "We need to celebrate with a special dinner together before I take you home." she smiled.

They were met at the door of her favorite restaurant by the manager. "You can't bring these Indians in here!" The man was nearly shouting as he barred the doorway. "Take them to the Chinese Restaurant down town. They might get in there, but they can't come in here!"

"And your sign is where?" she questioned as she pretended to look around. "You don't have a sign saying they can't come in, so we can legally come in." She tried to keep the fury she was feeling out of her voice but she couldn't.

Muttering and fussing he let them in, but his staff refused to serve them. Not wanting her guests to feel more hurt than they already were, she took them to the Chinese restaurant. She reached out and took one hand of each. "This hurts, and it is hard and unfair. Changes will come in the future generations. Always remember who you are and be strong. There are always people who care and understand at least a little of what your people have gone through in the past, and how hard your present lives are."

CHAPTER 25

One of the first things Rawhide had done after learning Johnny had left her his property was to hire workers to build the home, barns and fences. Since she had found Johnny's farm and house plans attached to the will, she was able to build everything almost exactly to his plans. She did add another house for a farm manager. Robby joked that when he grew up and took over the farm, she would have to live in the manager's house.

Once the building and fencing were completed it was time to purchase cattle. She and Robby began visiting cattle auctions to pick out some beef cattle. He wanted Herefords and Rawhide agreed with his choice. They were his cattle and young as he was, he knew this was going to be his farm someday.

The farm manager and his wife were already living happily in their new home by the time the herd of cattle arrived. Once the farm was up and running, she and Robby spent every weekend and holiday on the farm. Loving the country life, Robby often begged to stay with the manager and his family when school was out.

The lumber pile where Johnny had proposed to her was still there, half buried in weeds and greyed by the rain and sun. She had an arched roof built over it and planted flowers where the weeds had been. It was her special place, a memorial to the love they had for each other. She often went there for a quiet time after a hard week. Johnny's gift had touched her life, the lives of her family and many people who were too poor to have a voice. Being here in this spot always renewed her loving memories of him. Those memories gave her the courage to face what was often a trying work week.

It wasn't in Johnny's original building plans, but Rawhide had the builders make a spacious bedroom with an adjoining bathroom in the loft of the barn. She furnished it with a comfortable bed, an easy chair, a dresser with a mirror, and a soft rug on the floor.

In her work she met many people caught in situations where they needed a helping hand or a place to stay while they worked through difficult issues. That room was seldom empty for long. It had become a haven of safety and healing for many.

Sometimes she would pass Jack on the road and the old anger would flare up. She heard he was living on the farm he had cheated Awk out of. A self-crowned king of his ill-gotten kingdom, and doing well financially, from what she had heard.

"How do people like Jack get away with crime and come out looking like the good guy?" she muttered. Still, experiencing how Jack's evil mind worked had given her a great deal of success as a lawyer. She had learned that there were a lot of sleazy people like Jack. When she had a prospective client, her first words would be, "Unless you are willing to tell me the truth and the entire truth, I will not represent you. I will find every crack there is to find in your story."

****

Had he left well enough alone, Jack might have been able to live out the rest of his life as a free and wealthy man. As it was, he could not seem to resist an opportunity to cheat, steal, defraud and hurt the innocent, even if they were children. It was a bicycle scam that finally did him in.

If there were any problems of a legal nature in that farming community, they were brought to Rawhide. One such complaint was brought to her by her own son. Jack had sold a very good bicycle to one of Robby's friends for $10.00. Robby, who had grown up knowing what Jack had done to his Grandparents, wrote down the serial number of the bike and the physical description as well. The boy had the bike for a few days when Jack came back to the lad and told him he had found out that he had sold him a stolen bike. Out of the goodness of his heart, he was going to save the boy from paying a fine or going to jail by taking it to the police station himself. The frightened boy quickly gave him back the bike.

Robby visited another nearby town with the farm manager a few days later. He had become very good friends with a boy in that town as well and went along to spend time with his friend while the manager took care of some business. Robby found this friend riding a bike exactly like the one Jack had just taken back from his other friend. This friend said he had bought it from a man he did not know, for $10.00. Robby checked the number he had written in his little note pad with the serial number on the bike. It was the very same bike!

Rawhide went to the RCMP station and asked them to run a check to see if this bike had actually been stolen. It had been, along with fifteen others from almost the same neighborhood in the city. After a search for other victims, Rawhide soon learned that Jack was making a business of selling and then reclaiming these stolen bikes, only to resell them in another community. All the bikes were soon located and turned over to the police. Jack denied stealing them, saying the bikes had been dumped on his driveway. There were thirty upset boys that attested that Jack had told them the bikes were stolen and had taken them away from them. Jack was temporarily arrested, but released for lack of concrete evidence, although he was made to repay each boy.

Rawhide wasn't through with Jack yet. Something triggered her curiosity. She had never heard his last name until the bicycle fiasco, when The RCMP asked for his identification in her presence. He had always been known only as, "Jack". She shouldn't have been surprised that he did have a last name, but the fact he never used it made her curious. Jack had done a lot of evil things that she knew about. She wondered if he was hiding something even more sinister. She was determined to find out.

First, she called Eileen and asked her if she knew Jack's last name. She didn't. "Did your father pay Jack's wages by cheque?" was her next question.

"I don't think my father actually paid Jack regular wages," she replied. "I saw him hand Jack wads of bills sometimes. I have never found a record of anything else."

Acting on a hunch, Rawhide searched through Canadian birth and death records and found only one Jack Forster; born, November 7, 1890 in Ontario, deceased, early July, 1910 in the USA. No precise date was given for "Jack Forster's" death other than "early July". This man they knew as Jack came to work for Mr. Ardythe in July of that same year. Excited now, she searched everything she could find regarding Jack Forster. There was little about him. He had died while visiting a friend in the US. It was a suspected murder but unsolved.

There were two small clues for her to follow. The name of the one of the witness, (who had apparently witnessed nothing) was on the affidavit. There was also a name "Jonathon Quilllam" scribbled in a side note with nothing to explain why the name was there.

Her curiosity about Jonathon Quillam sent her to the local RCMP station once more.

"Well, Mrs Belker, I see you are honoring us with another visit. What can we do for you this morning? Constable Eric Agin at your service once again," he greeted as she entered the station.

Rawhide laughed. "I am only here for the second time in two weeks. I am looking for historical information on a man named Jonathon Quillam.

I am starting to think you should be a detective, not a lawyer. Do you have a personal reason for this search?

"Sort of personal. However, it is more than that. I think our bicycle thief is, in reality, a man named Jonathon Quillam."

Constable Agin began a search of the archives while she waited. Before long he pulled out a folder. "Here you go. We do have something here." He handed her a grainy old picture beside the name, "Jonathon Quillam." He was an American citizen, described as a dangerous fugitive. He had a long list of felony charges in the USA, including: extortion, assault with a deadly weapon, rape of an underage child and uttering threats. While awaiting trial he had escaped custody and had vanished without a trace.

She looked long at the picture. Jack was older now and a very heavy man, but an unmistakable mole showed in the picture that exactly matched the mole on his face. "Wonder why he didn't get it taken off. It would have been so easy," she muttered. "If I was a criminal, I would at least get rid of the obvious."

"I know you would, so please don't take up a life of crime," the officer smiled as she returned the file.

Was the man they knew as "Jack" really Jonathon Quillam masquerading as deceased Jack Forster? Rawhide happily gave the police the few documents she had located in her search. It would take a detective to follow through and find out the answers. Jack had Jack Forster's ID. At some point in time he had been in contact with the deceased man after his death as it was unlikely the man handed over his ID willingly. This was a was a major clue.

The detectives did their job well. The "witness who knew nothing" was still living and was located. He had been Jack Forster's best friend, the one the Canadian man was visiting. Jack had met a man named Jonathon Quillam at a baseball game on what was possibly the fateful day of his death. The friend said that Jonathon seemed like a nice and friendly person. He and Jack were close to the same age and seemed to really hit it off.

Jonathon mentioned he had a friend in Canada that he wanted to visit and wondered if Jack would take him there if he would pay the gas. Since this friend lived in Toronto as well, it was no inconvenience and Jack was delighted at the thought of spending time with his new friend on the long trip home. The last time anyone saw Jack alive, he was walking with Jonathon toward his car.

Nobody missed Jack Forster until several days later when he had not shown up for work as expected. Jack was found dead in the bushes near the baseball field a few days after he was reported missing. His car was found later, pushed into a ditch along a rural road.

There was nothing at the time for authorities to pin the murder on Jonathon Quillam. It was not until weeks later when his friend was questioned that anyone knew there was any connection between Jonathon Quillam, escaped US felon, and Jack Forster, deceased Canadian. Jonathon's name had been scribbled in the notes later, as a possible suspect and was wanted for questioning. But by that time Jonathon Quillam was nowhere to be found. Eventually the case went cold.

There was one question left to solve the puzzle. If this man was Jonathon Quilllam, how did he get from Ohio to Alberta, Canada?

When the police questioned Eileen, she was more than willing to tell what she knew. "My father went to Ohio to visit his brother right after my mother died. My father was a big fan of baseball, so he and his brother went to a game the afternoon before he started for home. After the game, the brothers went out together to have a bite to eat."

"A young man was waiting by the car when my father came out of the restaurant. He told my father he was from Toronto and had been here visiting a friend. His car had broken down. He couldn't wait for it to be repaired since he needed to get back to his job right away, but he had no means of getting home. He had seen the Canadian license on my father's car and politely asked if it was possible to get a ride back to Canada. So, my father gave him a ride. He really liked Jack and offered him a job as his manager if he would be willing to come west. Jack happily accepted, and he has been here ever since."

"Do you think your father ever questioned who Jack was, or wondered if he was hiding something?"

She shook her head "I am sure he didn't. Jack seemed nice and my father really liked him and depended on him a lot to build up "the community" the way he wanted it to be."

"Did no one ever connect the name Jack Forster to the murder of Jack Forster?" questioned the officer.

"Back then we did not hear much news from the east," replied Eileen. I don't think he ever used his last name. That is not uncommon around here. People often just go by their first names. This is the first time I have heard that name and I knew him for many years. Everybody just knew him as Jack."

****

It was a sultry summer afternoon with storm clouds building in the western sky. *Probably hail clouds,* Jack thought, content that his hay was cut and in the barns. His hired help did all the work. He had never done any menial labor. He was just glad he could find fools willing to work on a hot day like this. He filled a tall glass with his favorite "happy juice" and stretched out in a hammock on the veranda to relax. He had spent his lifetime hurting others, sometimes for his own gain, but mostly for the joy he found in seeing others suffer. He felt no remorse for the things he had done, only self-satisfaction over what he had gotten away with.

His huge grey tabby cat crawled up on his ample stomach. "I am one smart guy, kitty," he said as he stroked the cat's fur. I can do whatever I want to, and the police can't do a thing to me. That is because I am so much smarter than everyone else!" He smiled as he rocked slowly in the hammock. Soon the man and the cat were sound asleep. Life was indeed good for old Jack. He had made it rich without ever flexing his own muscles and he believed his shady past would never be uncovered after all these years.

****

Satisfied that they had found the fugitive criminal at last, the police pulled into his yard that afternoon. He was still on the veranda, sound asleep when they approached him.

"Jonathon Quillam?" He jumped up ready to fight at the sound of a name he had not heard for years.

"Put your hands up! You are under arrest for the suspected murder of Jack Forster."

He tried to run but for a man as heavy as he had become, a fast run was not an option. Within moments he was handcuffed and taken to the police car. Jack would never be back.

Rawhide felt life in the community was safer when "Jonathon Quillam" was arrested for the murder of a Canadian citizen. "May the real Jack Forster rest in peace," she sighed, "And may justice be served on Jonathon Quillam for all the evil he has done." She knew with the crimes he had committed, he would never be a free man again.

CHAPTER 26

Both Peter and Nataliya had been overjoyed at the news that the person they thought of as Jack had been arrested. He had brought them so much pain and suffering by what he had done to them. He was a murderer as well as a liar and a thief. He had not physically hurt anyone in the community for which they felt thankful. Alexander, who had to know everything about everything, soon learned from all the talk around him what the so called "Jack" had done to his parents. He became extra solicitous of both of them after that, but especially his father.

Although Peter would never be well again, he had been given medication that slowed the disease and left him more or less pain free. Nataliya's father had given him the Taxi car, which he was able to drive on his better days. His depression had lifted somewhat since he no longer had to leave the burden of earning a living all on Nataliya's shoulders. He seemed quite content, but Alexander was certain his father wanted to be back on his farm.

Rawhide was surprised one afternoon to look up and see her little brother standing in her office. "Why are you here, Alexander?" she asked, concern in her voice. "How did you get here?"

"Frank came this way for something today, and I came with him. I wanted to talk to you. I know you will think this is stupid, but I really want to buy the old homestead and farm it. I know that bog can be drained and then it could be the best land anywhere. Do you think you could loan me the money to buy it and drain the bog?"

Rawhide scratched her head. "You certainly are a determined little guy, aren't you? I am really going to have to think about that for a while. Let's go look at it together this weekend and talk it over."

Three days later the brother and sister were tramping over the old homestead. She had memories there, both sweet and bitter. All

Alex had was a burning desire to farm the land he was born on, even though he knew nothing about farming. After hours of walking all over the property, Rawhide wearily seated herself on an old stump and looked at her brother. "You know our parents made no money and were penniless here. Because of the Depression, false accusations and our father's illness they had no choice but to stay here, as they had nowhere to go. They had wanted to start a dairy farm, but they never could have succeeded because of so much boggy land. That bog hasn't changed. This is a worthless place, Alex. That is why no one has bought it yet."

"The bog is the very thing I want, sister. I have been studying about soil and if this was drained it could grow wonderful crops of vegetables that I could sell in the city. I have come out here a few times with some older friends and they have shown me where it can be drained. If you would buy it for me, lend me the money to pay for trenching a drainage ditch and a tractor, I will pay you back in a few years." He looked earnestly in his sister's face.

She finally relented. "OK. I will buy it for you and have it in your name, since it won't cost much. It might be worth something some-day, so we will call it an investment. I won't lend you money to drain the swamp though. You are too young to know what you want. If you still have this idea after you grow up, we'll talk then." She chucked her little brother under the chin and led the way back to her car. Making good on her promise, she paid the back taxes on the land. After show-ing Alexander his land title at least six more times, she filed it away for safekeeping. She had a feeling of attachment to the place as well. That was the only reason her brother talked her into buying it. She was quite sure her parents wanted nothing more to do with it!

****

Eileen continued to work with the farmers to get more of them to re-finance through the banks. Of course, this transition created its share of legal challenges and she enlisted Rawhide's help. Rather than work from the city on these issues, Rawhide set up a what she thought was a temporary local office.

With the burgeoning prosperity of the 1950's, the town was booming and becoming a small city. Rawhide soon made a decision to close her city office and set up her practice in this more rural setting. There was more than enough legal work to be done at a local level and her reputation had followed her. She was only a phone call away if a prospective client from the city needed her services.

The decision to leave the city had advantages. She could make her permanent home on the farm Johnny had left her. She appreciated the short drives down the quiet country road between her home and office, with no city traffic to battle. She felt her life was about as good as it could get.

As for Robby, there was nothing that could have brought him more joy than the decision to live on, "his farm." It was his dream come true! Watching Robby as he played with the baby calves, finding him rejoicing over a new born colt or munching a fistful of freshly pulled carrots from the garden, Rawhide knew she had made the right choice for Robby's sake.

CHAPTER 27

The rodeo was finished. The weather had been scorching hot and the clown felt exhausted after a hard day of rescuing bull riders and fallen cowboys. He wanted nothing more than to find a quiet country road where he could escape the heat and noise of the rodeo. In the country he could take the mask off his scarred and gnarled face and feel cooling fresh air on his skin. Maybe he could even find a farmer kind enough to let him sleep in his barn.

Rawhide was on her way home from work when she saw a figure on the road ahead. During the depression there had been a lot of hoboes that had ridden the rails to the towns and then would go to nearby farms, looking for work or food. She had seen several as she walked to school as a girl. It had been years since she had seen one around anywhere, but this poor man looked like he might have been riding the rails for a long time. He certainly was ragged and dirty.

She pulled up beside him. "Do you live around here? I don't think I have seen you around before."

He kept walking as he spoke, "I guess you could say I am from all over. I am a rodeo clown and I follow the rodeos. The one here just finished. I have a few days to relax before moving onto the next one. I used to be a farm boy, so I wanted to visit a farm or two while I am here."

She was driving slowly beside him. "I live right up the road on a farm. I also have a guest room in the barn. If you have no place else to stay you are welcome to stay there since it is empty right now. You can come and go as you please. I am going there now, if you would care for a ride."

He hesitated before he spoke. "That is a kind offer. I am tired and the thought of that room is tempting. I will only stay for three days and I promise I won't get in your way. Thank you, Miss, uh?"

"Just call me Rawhide."

He was soon settled in the cozy barn room. He enjoyed a hot shower and was about to sink into the plush comfort of the bed when there was a knock on the door and a child's voice shouting, "Mother asks if you would like to eat with us."

Happy to accept, he followed the boy to the house. The meal was the best he had eaten for a long time. This woman was certainly a good cook, but the boy would not stop asking him questions.

Robby helped himself to a second piece of apple pie. "What happened to your face, Mister? You look weird. Sort of like you are some kind of a turtle." He eyed the scarred man as closely as he could without actually getting in his space.

"I told you I was a clown and clowns just look funny," the man replied

"Were you born a clown," Robby was persistent.

"I didn't see myself when I was born so you will have to ask my mother that question. Now I am really tired. Thank you Miss,uh, Rawhide, for the meal." He almost ran back to the barn to escape any more of Robby's endless questions. It hurt to be reminded of his deformities

He said he could stay for three days before he would have to move on. It would be hard to stay that long and face Robby's endless questions. He countered this the next day by following the boy around and asking questions, to the boy's great annoyance.

"Mother!" Robby shouted when she arrived home from work the second evening. "Get rid of this guy and stop bringing bums like this home. I can't stand him following me around all the time. You have brought some weirdos home before, but this one is too much. Don't you ever think you might have bought a criminal home and he might hurt us?"

"There is always a possibility someone might hurt us. Somehow, I don't think someone who is that down and out is as dangerous as you think he might be," she responded. "I agree this guy is ugly to look at. Just because he is scarred does not mean he is not a nice person though. Whatever happened, he has suffered a lot and I am asking you to be kind to him." She handed Robby a bag of groceries to carry and followed him to the house with another bag in her arms.

"He won't be here long anyway Robby" she continued as she prepared the evening meal." Like I said, we have no idea what he has been through and it is terribly rude of you to ask him those questions about how he looks. I find him really pleasant to talk to and I think he needs friends. So, go and invite him to dinner now and if you ask him anything about his looks again, I will send you to your room like a two-year-old!"

Things went well to begin with. Bobby politely asked about rodeos, and then the man asked Rawhide what type of work she did.

Robby answered the question before she had a chance to speak. "My Mom's a lawyer. She helps people even if they can't pay her, so if you are a bum or something and you are in trouble, she will help you for free. She is really smart and has put some bad people in jail. If you are a bad person, she will find out about it and she will get you, just like she got Jack!"

The boy stopped just in time to catch an ominous look from his mother. "Excuse me. I think I need to finish my chores. Right now!" he said as he jumped up from the table.

Rawhide sighed. "Lawyers' children pick up too much. I apologize for his rudeness. I think maybe I have been doing too much lawyering and not enough mothering!"

"Not to worry," the scarred man responded with a chuckle. "I have been following him around all day and annoying him too." He changed the subject quickly. "You have a real nice place here, lady. I like the way you planned everything out, especially that guest room. I can't begin to tell you how good it has felt to be in that haven you created for others."

"Thank you," she responded, "This is a special place to me. I call it Johnny's Place." She said no more, and the man soon excused himself and left.

The next evening when she arrived home, she found the man teaching Robby how to lasso a post with Frank and Alex watching and cheering Robby on. She had barely opened her car door when Alex was begging her to go with him to the homestead.

"Little Brother, you are such a pest," she laughed, sliding out of the car and giving him a hug. "Wow! Just look at you! You are way taller than me already! What have you been eating? Anyway, to answer your question. It is a pleasant evening for a ride so while I make sandwiches, you and Robby get the horses saddled. Find out if our guest can ride and if he does, invite him along, please."

She was busy making the lunch when she looked up to see Frank and her farm manager standing outside the screen door. Quickly washing her hands, she went to the door and asked them in.

Her manager wasted no time. "After I told you I was having health problems and would have to quit, you asked me to try to find someone to take my place. This man you have staying in the barn is exactly the person you need. He is kind of hard to look at but looks don't mean a thing on this job. He has been working along with me the past couple of days and he certainly knows what he is doing when it comes to farming! "

"I have been watching him all afternoon as well," added Frank. "You could search the whole world over and not find a man better at the job than he is. I think he is the answer to your dilemma and he certainly could use the work, and a home to live in, rather than trying to survive as a rodeo clown."

"I never thought of him as a farm manager, but I do trust the judgement of you two. We need someone very soon, so I will ask him if he wants the job. I think he had his heart set on leaving tomorrow, so he might not be interested, but it never hurts to try."

The summer had been unusually dry. As they rode along the horse's hooves kicked up little poofs of dust. Grasshoppers, startled by their approach flew high in the air, making a scratching sound before landing. The smells and sounds of the forest in the warm late afternoon air added to the peace of the ride. She loved the tranquility and stillness of the forest.

Frank and the two boys had raced on ahead, leaving Rawhide and her guest going at a much easier pace. She turned to him. "I apologize that I never asked you your name. I am sure you have a title beyond being called clown."

"Well, Robby has been quite content calling me "the bum" until this afternoon. I think we have a truce of sorts in place now, so now I guess I can be considered worthy of being called by my own name! I should have introduced myself before. My name is Richard," he responded.

"I don't want to be as inquisitive as Robby, but your injuries are obvious. Are you comfortable sharing what happened?"

They rode on in silence for quite some time before he spoke. "I find it hard to talk about what happened to me. There are memories I wish would go away, but they never will. I was in the war and our plane was shot down. I was the pilot and somehow survived the crash with mainly just facial burns and multiple fractures. My best friend was the gunner. He didn't make it. I grieved over his death, but I was in such pain I wondered if he were not better off than I was."

"That has to be so hard. I can only imagine what you have gone through." Her voice was soft with compassion.

Once more they rode on in silence, the warm air wrapping them in a comfortable cloak. "My fiancé was in the war as well," she said at last. "We used to walk together down this very road when we went to school,"

It was Richard's turn to question her. "You say fiancé? Is he one of us who gave his life over there? What was his name? A lot of us Canadian guys were posted together, and I just might have known him."

"His name was Johnny Carpenter," There was more than a tinge of sadness in her voice.

"I did know him. He was reported MIA during the Battle of Pearl Harbor if I recall correctly," he responded sadly, noting the tears that slid down her face. She must have cared for him deeply.

She took a deep breath. "This is a change of subject, but my farm manager is not well and needs to leave. The work is becoming far too heavy for him. Both he and Frank suggested that I ask you to take over the job. You will have to be able to run the place on your own as I am very involved in my work and have little time to worry about the everyday issues of farming. If you are interested and can do that, the job is yours as soon as the present manager leaves."

"Ma'm, I would be more than happy to take the job. I have always liked farming and I would appreciate this chance to work for you here. I will do my best not to disappoint you."

Moments later they arrived at the Homestead. The drought had been long, so they could ride safely in the boggy meadow. Frank, Richard and Alex went exploring while Rawhide set out the picnic meal. They returned with Alex more exuberant than ever, but he waited until the meal was over before he shared his excitement with her.

As he swallowed the last bite, he spoke. "Rawhide, our parents are not getting younger. Mother goes to work in that hot kitchen every day just to basically survive. She is not going to be able to do that forever. Then what? You know she is a person who loves freedom and the great outdoors. Father drives the taxi sometimes and it makes him feel better about himself. In spite of everything those two have gone through on this place, they have this dream of coming back with their son, me. I know you think I am too young, but I am going to have our father and mother here. Richard has promised to help me, and so has Frank.

Rawhide started to speak, but he interrupted. "We are their children and their health and happiness are our responsibility. Since Grandpa and Grandma Burak moved to Toronto, our parents want to come back here all the more."

Once again Rawhide tried to speak. He held his hand up. "I'm not done yet, Sister. Frank and Richard both know a lot about land and agree that with proper drainage this soil would raise wonderful vegetable crops. They said if we made a lake at the far end where it is very low the higher part could be drained into the lake. The best part is that Frank has a friend that will loan him his equipment. Both Frank and this man, (he pointed at Richard), know how to run it, so it would only cost the fuel."

"And then what?" asked Rawhide, feeling that she was being over ruled. Her brother was only twelve. Far too young for such great ideas.

"As soon as the drainage is in, I need a tractor to work it up, so I can start growing vegetables next year. Probably only potatoes the first year. Frank says he can make me a big root cellar in the side hill at the same time he is making the lake and canal. That way I can store vegetables like potatoes and carrots."

All eyes were on her as she gathered up the remnants of the picnic. "I think we better get home before dark," was her only response.

Richard rode beside her on the way home. "I know you think he is too young, Rawhide, but farm boys start young. I grew up doing farm work with my father and it was fun. These boys have dreams and will work toward them along with the men who will help them. Frank is willing to help Alex get started and if I am your farm manager, I will be there working along with the boys all the time. From what Alex says, your parents are behind this."

Rawhide was silent for the rest of the ride home. As she got off her horse, she said briefly, "I will think about it, Richard. This is too much all at once. He is only twelve years old."

Early the following morning she found her manager and let him know she had followed his advice to hire Richard. He responded with enthusiasm. "That was a wise decision! If you hire that guy, you'll never be sorry you did. He can start as soon as he wants to, but I will need a couple of weeks before I move out, if that is alright with you."

Rawhide smiled. "Of course. Stay as long as you need to. I am paying you for the entire month though. You deserve it! I hope your replacement can measure up to your faith in him. You have done a great job managing this farm. I can't thank you enough!"

CHAPTER 28

Work on Alex's project proceeded quickly. Within two weeks the lake was completed, and the canal dug the following week. The man who had loaned the equipment to Frank had a tractor that he offered to sell the boy at a low price. Rawhide eventually relented and bought him the tractor.

No one was home one evening when she came home. Curious, she drove her car down the bumpy road to the homestead to see if everyone was there. The first person she saw was her mother standing by the old pole barn. The next thing she saw was a large pile of lumber.

"What are you doing here, Mother?" she asked in surprise.

"Your father and I moved here today!" Nataliya enthused. "I sold my home and had enough equity to buy the lumber for a new house. Frank, Richard and the boys are going to build it. Your father has designed it and he is going to oversee the building."

Rawhide looked down where the boggy grass meadows had been. Instead of just tall waving grass, she saw a large patch of rich black earth, ploughed and waiting for winter frosts to mellow it before it would be planted the following spring. Laughing, she realized he had used the little plough that was still on the homestead, to plough the field. She mentally applauded her brother for his tenacity in doing a big job with next to nothing. He was going to need some better equipment though if he was serious about this idea of his.

Alex was with the others, putting in the foundation for the new home. Alex, her baby brother! He would soon be as tall as their father. When had he become a man? There was Robby, another young man. They weren't her babies any more and she had to set them free to be men. It had happened too fast and she wasn't ready to let them go yet.

She turned to her mother. "You need to come and stay with me until your new home is ready. That is going to take a while."

Nataliya hugged her daughter. "No. I have cleaned out the dug-out home and put new grass in the beds. Your father and I are actually looking forward to living in it again. She was smiling now, with almost youthful joy. "We are home again, and we have both a daughter and a son now!"

Richard and Robby rode home with her. Alex insisted on staying with their parents, overjoyed to be able to sleep in the little dirt home he had been born in.

Robby left quickly after that evening meal. Richard lingered. "I want to thank you, Rawhide for a chance at this job. You have done a great job raising those two young men. I am going to enjoy working with both of them."

"I want to thank you too, Richard, for what you are doing for them. Never mind the few tears you see me cry. They were my babies. They are growing up too fast and pretty soon they won't need me. But they needed a man in their life and in these past weeks I have seen a big difference in them."

"Ma'm, the way you cook they will still be home for meals for a long time. Thank you for another of your wonderful meals."

She smiled. "You are welcome. By the way", she continued, "The manager and his family left today, and you can move in tonight if it is clean. If you come with me, we can check it out. You can move in immediately if it is ready."

"Now it is my turn to ask personal questions," he said as they walked together to the manager's house. "I know that Alex is your brother, but who is Robby? I have seen a lot of people come and go, but where is your husband?" He looked at her quizzically.

She sighed. "You got scarred in a plane crash. I have gone through my own war. I have scars too, but they don't show on the outside. My father tried to talk me into marrying a man that I did not like as this man offered to trade land for me. My father is not a terrible person, but he was ill and desperate to make a living and have a decent home for my mother who was expecting Alex at the time. Some people in this community were very unkind to my father and also ruined his reputation by spreading lies about him. He suffered a lot from that, as it made it so he could not find work to support us. On top of that, he had been ill for years.

My father thought what this man, Awk, offered in exchange for me sounded like a good deal for everyone. I would be safely married off to a rich man and father would be able to have a decent living and a home. When I refused, my father set a trap so that this man could rape me. I got pregnant and was then forced to marry Awk. Bobby is my son from that situation.

Awk was seldom home. When he did come home, he would yell at me and call me a lot of cruel names. I was always glad to see him leave. I always lived with fear, not knowing when he would be back. Once he beat me very badly for using his money stash to buy feed for his cattle and take Alex to the doctor.

Awk drank and gambled almost continuously. In the end, he died of liver problems. He was penniless by this time, having gambled away everything he ever owned. I found out before he died that he was the half-brother of my fiancé. There is a lot more to the story but that is enough to answer your question. It is not something I like to talk about."

Richard shook his head but said nothing.

The house had been left in spotless condition. Richard moved in immediately. He thought of the many nights he had slept on the cold ground, wondering if there would ever be a place of comfort again. The rodeo life was hard, barely earning him enough to buy food. He was too marred to even be a clown unless he wore a mask and a wig, and it made him feel sub-human. Winters were the worst. Sometimes he could earn a little cleaning horse barns, and he could sleep in the barns. He had tried not to think of the soft beds and warm blankets in his mother's home. There was a life before the war when he was good looking, popular, knew what he wanted and where he was going in life. There was a different life now. He was alone and living a life he had never dreamed of having to live. Until now, that is.

That flash of fire during the crash had changed his life in a moment. From then on he had no choice but drudging out an existence with no future as far as he could see. He had been dreading the thought of another winter. This job was a lifesaver! After a shower he slid into the soft covers, hoping that if this was a dream it would never end. What had once been a life full of dreams had been reduced to being happy just to have enough food, a roof over his head and warm blankets to cover him while he slept

CHAPTER 29

There were other advantages to having Richard there, Rawhide soon realized. She often had to stay in the city because of court cases. It wasn't a problem for her personally, as Eileen and Frank kept the basement suite open for her. It was hard on Robby though. She always had to take him out of school except on rare occasions when the former manager and his wife could keep him for a few days. Now that Richard was there, she could leave, knowing her son was happy and well cared for. Robby no longer thought of Richard as ugly. He called him "Uncle" out of respect and said he was the best friend he ever had.

Her parents were settled in their new home and Rawhide noted with joy that her father's depression was completely gone. The loving "Daddy" she once knew was back! Her parents still loved to sing together and now that they were accepted as part of the community, were often asked to sing in churches and for weddings. They were the "Romanovs" now, not "The Bohunks from the Swamp,"

Peter, with the help of Alex, had found a career. He was gifted in architecture, but his stiff hands prevented him from drafting his plans. Instead he explained the designs to Alex, measurement by measurement, and Alex drew the plans. He began marketing the plans as well. He had never been a farmer, but he found fulfillment at last in using his own gifts. It was not long before people were calling on "The Big Rus" to help them design new homes or plans for renovations.

Rawhide's own life was changing. Aside from playing while she was in school, Rawhide had never played games in her entire life. Now she would often come home and find Richard playing games with the boys. It wasn't long until she found herself being enticed into games of tag, hide and seek, scrub and best of all, foot races, something she always won! In the winter, Richard and the boys made a skating rink behind the barn. She put on skates for the first time and, hand in hand, Richard helped her learn to skate. It wasn't long before they involved her in playing shinny. During the winter evenings, Richard and Robby pulled out the trove of board games they had bought. The three would curl up by her fireplace sipping hot chocolate and playing until Robby had to go to bed. After he left, Rawhide and Richard would sit, enjoying another cup of hot chocolate. They enjoyed each other's company and had endless conversations about their days work and the world in general.

"You are very beautiful," he stated suddenly one evening while they were in the middle of discussing legal practices. "Yes, your fiancé was lost in the war and you were married to a cruel, broken person, but I am puzzled that you have not found someone else? That was many years ago."

She laughed a little, "Well, there was someone else for a while. Sort of that is. His name was Jason. We dated off and on while I was in law school, but somehow it never seemed to click for me. He came from a rich family and his mother called me a peasant because I expressed my own views on "equal opportunity". It was kind of a bad scene and Jason and I broke up. Two days later I found that my fiancé had willed me this farm and much more. Of course, dear Jason immediately wanted us to get back together as soon as he got wind of my new fortune and was planning on taking over everything. He wanted to tell me where to invest, and pretty much how to live my life. I realized then why nothing had really clicked for me with Jason. Johnny was never that way. He loved me the way I was without any thought of controlling me. I guess I could say, I have been in love with Johnny since I was a little girl. There is no one to take his place in my heart."

She looked in the fire for a few minutes. "My parents hid the letters that Johnny had sent me. I had never heard from him after he left to go fight in the war. Later, I found his letters. I keep them right here. Do you mind if I read you what he wrote in his very last letter?" She pulled the letter from a box on the mantle and read the words, "No matter what happens to me, no matter what happens to you, I will always take care of you, Little Rawhide. Be strong."

Placing the letter back in its safe place she sat down again. "All that time, Johnny was thinking of me and left all he had for me. He has taken care of me just like he said he would. Because of his legacy, I have been able to help others. It is because of his gift that I have this place and the guest room in the barn. It was Johnny that provided you with a place to stay, and now a job. Indirectly, having you here is a gift from Johnny too. I know this must sound strange but even though Johnny is dead, I would feel as if I would be just wrong, if I married someone else." She had tears in her eyes as she spoke.

She rose, "Anyway, I have a big court case tomorrow, and I need my sleep." She went with him to the door and watched as he walked into the darkness.

After game playing a few nights later, she said, "I am always talking about me and my sorrow over losing Johnny. What about you? Did you have a girlfriend before you went to war?"

There was a long silence before he answered. "Yes," he finally responded. "All of us soldier boys had girlfriends waiting for us back home. It kept us sane, waiting for letters and packages." There was another long silence. He sighed deeply but she wondered if it was a little sob instead. "War changes everything. Many of the boys gave their lives. The wounded ones often have to lay our dreams down to rust- among our medals. There is not much else to say. I could not go back and let her see me this way."

She saw tears running down his cheeks. "Thank you for giving so much for our freedom", she said softly.

"I need to go, Rawhide. There are places a wounded soldier should never let his mind go and I did. I am sorry." He rose and went out the door without another word.

Back in his house, Richard threw himself on the bed and cried like a child. Was giving up all his dreams and being on the outside edge of society for the rest of his life worth it? He came back from that war a broken thing with no place to fit in, no hope for a normal life. He was ugly. Just ugly.

****

Spring came, and the family all turned out to help Alex plant potatoes. "This is the last year I will need much help because Father designed a potato planter and digger," he proudly told his sister. "Richard is going to make it as soon as father and I get the plans made."

Rawhide looked over at Richard who was digging holes with a shovel for Alex to drop the potato seed in. "You are so full of surprises! Is there anything you can't do, Richard? Seriously I don't know what these boys would do without you. In fact, I don't know how any of us would manage without you. You seem to be the one that keeps everything in place and moving forward. Have I ever told you how much I appreciate you being here?"

He smiled as best he could with his leathery lips. "Well, you feed me once in a while, so I thought maybe you found me useful around the farm," he said, and went on planting as if her words had not just made his heart soar to the clouds. It was wonderful to feel accepted again after his years of wandering and being unwanted.

That evening Robby stayed on the homestead. Rawhide had to be at work in the morning and since Robby wanted the truck, she was going to walk through the forested shortcut. Richard came with her, "In case something wants to eat her, I will go along to fight it off," he had told her mother after she asked him to stay for the night.

Rawhide laughed. "I wonder if I look like animal food or something? Johnny always walked with me to protect me from the 'lions and the tigers.' What are you protecting me from?"

"Probably from tripping over roots in the dark and breaking bones," he chuckled as he caught her as she tripped over a root in the path.

They laughed together. As she walked beside him through the rapidly darkening evening, she realized that with Richard beside her, she felt safe and protected even though there was nothing to be protected from. It was just that Richard was so caring of everyone, including herself. He had done so much for the boys. It filled her with pride as she watched Robby proudly doing the work of a man, and Alex getting his dream in place and being the son that their parents always wanted. With Johnny's gift, the lad was giving their parents a home and a great deal of happiness. Johnny's gift had helped many people. Richard was a definite part of Johnny's gift. Not only was he a great farm manager and a father figure to her boys, he had brought happiness into her own life. She felt proud to be accepted as his friend.

****

It was the end of a difficult week for Rawhide. She had taken on a Pro Bono case for a very poor couple, and with her usual tenacity had done a lot of homework before taking the case. Although she had won the case, it seemed nothing could be changed in the lives of the couple. There were three generations that had lived in poverty, not seeing any way out. Poor white trash, as they were referred to by many; they had experienced many put downs and a lack of opportunity. They were locked in a sense of apathy, hopelessness and despair. They had a son almost the same age as her boys, who spent most of his time roaming the streets. There are still hopes and dreams in the mind of the young; a chance to move ahead and in doing so lift others from the crippling despair. She wondered how Richard would feel if she invited this boy to be with him as another "helper"

She couldn't find Richard or Robby when she arrived home. She thought they were probably at the homestead. She was too tired to go there herself. Instead she went to the place she called the "shrine" to sit on the lumber pile and let her mind go back to the sweet innocent memories of Johnny.

She was both surprised and happy to find Richard sitting there. "Well, hi there!" she said as she seated herself on the pile. "I am glad to find you here since I wanted to talk to you about something. You are free to say 'No' if you don't want to do it, so don't feel pressured. There is this boy named Leroy that I met. He is about Robby's and Alex's age. His parents have been going through a hard time for their entire lives, and this lad has no place to fit in either at home or in public. It made me think of Awk somehow, and how his life might have been different if someone had given him a dream of what life could be. You are so good with the other boys, so I am wondering if I brought him here, could you take him in and teach him like you are doing with our boys?"

He caught his breath. She had said, "Our boys" and his heart jumped. His voice was shaky as he replied, "I can certainly give it a try if you think it will help the lad." He felt again like she had accepted him as part of a team. It felt so good to the wounded soldier to be part of something again. It wasn't family but it was close.

"We can only try. Thank you." She smiled. "Each child that has a dream has a road ahead. I think you are good at helping boys dream and follow their dreams. Perhaps you had to give up your own dreams, but you are so good at inspiring others to dream and reach high."

Her words made his heart sing. Yes, she seemed to see him as a whole person with worth. They sat in a friendly silence, both enjoying the company of the other in the warm evening. He broke the silence with a question. "Is there a special meaning to this old pile of lumber with an arch over it and all the flowers? Most people burn old piles, not make them into a place of beauty like this."

"This is my most special place, Richard. The day Johnny asked me to be his wife he had led me here to show me his land and the lumber he had already purchased to begin our home. This is where he asked me to marry him. He gave me a ring to wear on a chain around my neck and he had one around his neck. I still wear mine. It sounds silly, but I think I will spend my life waiting for him to come back, even though I know he won't. My heart won't let me stop loving him."

Richard turned a little, so he could see her face. "If you found someone you could love as much as Johnny, do you think you could let Johnny go, and move on with someone new? If Johnny loved you enough to give you all this, he would love you enough to want to set your heart free, don't you think? He would not want to think of you growing old alone."

She rose to go as she answered. "I do think Johnny would want me to move on. I am the problem. I am just not sure I could ever let him go out of my heart and it wouldn't be fair to another man if I couldn't let my Johnny go."

He sat alone on the lumber pile for a long time before going back to his house. He had a home and a job. It was the best he could hope for. This beautiful woman saw him as a friend and an equal and that was good. He knew that was all it could ever be. He was thankful, but his heart ached just the same. How he wished he could tell Rawhide, the woman who was so loyal to Johnny, that he was in love with her. He had truly given up a lifetime of love so that he could fight in that war.

Chapter 30

It was a beautiful afternoon in early October. Begging a week off school, the three boys had been harvesting the potato crop from morning to night. The digger worked well, but it still needed people to pick the potatoes up. Richard was promising innovations so that everything ould be done by the machine next fall, but for now it was a job to do by hand. Robby and Leroy had worked with Alex picking up the gleaming tubers. Richard helped when he could, and even Nataliya was out at times, racing with the boys to see who could pick potatoes the fastest. Rawhide came out to help, as well, on the last day of harvest. She went to the root cellar, rejoicing over the perfect potatoes and feeling proud of her little brother. He had contracts with several restaurants in the city and a couple in the local town. He could sell every potato he had and make a good profit.

She looked at how little had been planted compared to the many acres he could use. There was a definite possibility of a big income, but as she straightened her aching back, she knew it had to be more than just a family project if he was going to use all that land.

She found her beaming brother cleaning the digger before putting it away. "We need to talk some business, Little Brother," she said. "You need to have a plan in place as to how you are going to seed, cultivate, weed and harvest this project of yours. Yes, we all helped you this time, but your project is greater than this family's ability or time. What are you planning for the future?"

He looked up with a grin on his dusty face. "You worry so much, Big Sister. You know how you always figure things out? I can do that too, and I have everything taken care of! Leroy and I are going to be partners. For planting, weeding, and harvest, he knows enough kids that need to have jobs. Mother has agreed to cook when we have our workers here. Richard has promised some great baseball games with the kids after work too. There is a nice place where they can put up tents and camp while they are here. I think it will be more fun than work!"

He tossed some sod out of his digger. "There are a few more things you don't know, Sister. Leroy and I found a nice house in town for his parents to rent. Leroy's mother likes to cook, and our mother is going to help her get started since she had a lot of experience working in the hospital kitchen. They can rent the old café for almost nothing. Leroy's father can pound nails, so he and our father have teamed up. Our father will do the planning and supervise the job while Leroy's father will do the actual renovations. Leroy and I will be helping them after the potato crop is harvested and we have the fields cultivated.

Father and Leroy's father are also doing renovations for other people when they are finished with the café. They have two contracts already."

She looked at her brother in disbelief. "When did all this happen without me even knowing?" she asked. "Somebody told me the old café was being renovated but I had no idea my own family was involved in this. I didn't even bother to drive across town to see what was going on."

"While you were so busy seeing that bad guys go to jail and the good guys go free, your baby brother has been busy too," he laughed.

She pinched his nose like old times. "How did you grow up so fast and so smart anyway?"

"The same way you did. By eating our mother's good cooking. I'm pretty sure it was either the perogies or the cabbage rolls that did it! I smell food cooking now, and I am starving!"

They walked arm in arm to where their mother was cooking over an open fire, with potatoes roasting in the coals. The meal was not ready yet, so Rawhide walked to the old pole barn, sat down and propped herself against the south side, something she had often done as a child when she needed to think things through. In nature, little had changed. The gold and yellow of the birch trees still contrasted with the dark green spruce and the brown and yellow leaves of poplar and the red of the highbush cranberry bushes.

The forest view might be the same, but time and circumstances had changed her own life to a totally different landscape. The child no longer existed and had been replaced by her adult self, carved from the circumstances that had been part of her life. She thought of Johnny and the pure sweet innocence of being in love as a child. It hit her like a jolt as she realized she could never be in love that way again. Johnny was gone and so was the child she used to be. She wondered what love really was. She thought of her parents who had rebuilt a relationship that had seemed forever shattered. Their lives had changed but in the mellow relationship they had now, she sensed a much deeper love had taken the place of their younger dreams. She thought of her grandparents who had been separated for so many heartbreaking years. They were now rejoicing, living each day they had left together as a gift.

Richard. She thought of him a lot and wondered if he meant more to her than just a friend. She liked being with him; she had missed and thought of him all day. It had been fun working with the family but there was that emptiness because Richard wasn't there.

With Leroy to help him, Richard had gone to the city to deliver the first truck load of potatoes. Rawhide found it delightful to watch Leroy gain confidence and the time he spent with Richard was helping him see potential in what he could do. With Richard's encouragement and his parent's permission, Leroy began attending the same school her boys were. The comradery between the boys and Richard was obvious and going to a new school where he had friends already gave him an inroad to a successful social life in school. Richard was teaching the boys to have fun while they worked and to always have a goal to work toward. She expected Leroy would be spending much of his time on the farm, but with his parents living nearby he would have the best of both worlds.

As Richard drove in the yard with the now empty truck, she walked to meet him. As soon as the truck stopped, Leroy jumped out and raced to join his two new friends while Richard walked to where she waited for him. Together, they watched the three boys wrestling. "I can't believe they still have the energy to wrestle after a hard day of work! I am beat!' Richard groaned, rubbing his shoulders. Looking at Rawhide's mud caked jeans and her stained hands, he laughed. "I can see you have been doing your share of work too, or else you were playing in the dirt all day. You look like a farmer!"

"I prefer being a peasant rather than a farmer," she laughed. "It just has a more warm and earthy sound to it."

"Whatever works best for you! Are you ready to go home yet, peasant woman? If you are, I will pull Robby away from his friends and we will be on our way."

She shook her head. My Mother and Father are roasting potatoes and who knows what else they are cooking on their bonfire. They wouldn't be too happy if we left the celebration now!" She brought him a cool drink of water. "Here, rest for a bit while I help Mother with the meal. We will call you when it is ready."

Gratefully, he took the drink from her hands and sank down on the soft, sun warmed earth. The war had taken so much from him but being employed by someone as kind as Rawhide filled some of the loneliness in his heart. He dozed peacefully until Alexander called him for supper.

The boys ate ravenously, declaring fire roasted potatoes as the best food and convincing Leroy he had to eat more so he could catch up to them in height. Both of them were close to six feet tall by now, but poor Leroy was much shorter. He good naturedly ate all they put on his plate. Richard reassured him that everyone grows at a different speed, and he might end up the tallest in the end. Even if he didn't get tall, he would be just the right height for himself so not to worry.

The boys were still bursting with energy after the meal and engaged in a potato fight with the small potatoes. "Wonder where they get so much energy from", sighed Nataliya, rubbing her back.

Rawhide laughed. "From what Grandma Burak says about you when you were young, we can be glad the boys are as calm and quiet as they are!"

Nataliya smiled a far away smile. "Age changes everything, I guess. I haven't climbed a tree or jumped off buildings in years and I don't plan to do things like that anytime soon either.

Giving her mother a hug, Rawhide busied herself with washing dishes. "Probably raising you gave your mother experience in going through hard experiences when she had to. They both smiled, knowing that Natalya might have been a hard child to raise because she was so strong minded, yet it was that same determination that had kept her going through some very hard years.

Nataliya and Rawhide were just washing the last of the dishes when Richard joined them, "Do you think us two old people have the strength to walk home tonight, as tired as we are? I guess Robby and

Leroy forgot you came on the truck with us this morning and don't have your car here. They just took off with the truck leaving us no choice but to walk home. I will promise to protect you from all the roots and rocks that will rise up and trip you on the way home, Fair Lady," he said, bowing to her.

Putting the last of the dishes away, she hugged her parents and stepped out into the crisp autumn evening. She had carelessly tossed her jacket in the truck while they were feasting by the bonfire. The air had grown chilly now, and she hugged herself to try to keep warm. Richard noticed and without a word draped his warm jacket around her shoulders.

Her heart had been in a turmoil all day. Her mind went over the list of things that she liked about him. He was kind and thoughtful to everyone. He looked for ways to help others, but not intrusively. He was a father to her boys. He respected the rights of everyone. He had brought a great deal of peace and security to her own life and she always looked forward to spending time with him. Was this love? The trouble was that It was nothing like she had felt for Johnny when she was full of dreams and hopes, with no thought of life being anything but perfect. No, she didn't feel like that at all.

Wrapped in the shelter and warmth of his jacket she fully realized at last that what she felt for him was far deeper than any simple friendship. She wanted him in her life forever! She reached for his hand and gave it a little squeeze. He thought his heart would burst. He hoped she would not pull her hand away, and she didn't.

"Thank you for the coat, Richard. We had better run home fast, so you don't get cold." But they didn't run. Instead they stopped walking and stood, looking at each other. "I missed you so much while you were gone today," she went on. "When I am away at work do you ever miss me and look forward to me coming back?"

"I always miss you, Rawhide" he said, his voice husky with emotion. "When you come home it brightens everybody's day, but mine most of all."

"I realized while you were gone today that I never want to be without you in my life," she whispered.

"Does that mean you want a life contract for me to work for you, or do you actually mean you want to be in my life forever as my wife?" he asked.

"I really like you Richard, I have for a long time. Today I realized I love you and only you. I want to be part of your life as your wife. You are the only person that can fill the empty spot where Johnny used to be."

He moaned softly. "Rawhide, I have loved you since the very first day I saw you, but I am so ugly it would be wrong for me to even think of being married to you. I can't ask you to spend your life with me. That would be too big a sacrifice for you to make. It just would not be right for someone like you to marry someone like me."

She pulled her hand from his and faced him. "Richard, I don't see scars when I look at you. I only see the kind, caring wonderful man that you are. You are my best friend and you are the man that has stolen my heart without even trying, without me even realizing you had, until this afternoon. I can't imagine my life without you being part of it forever.

Tears were running down his cheeks as he whispered, "I want nothing more in this world than to be your husband." He pulled her into his arms. "You are so beautiful, but I don't even look human any more. What will people say about you if you throw your life away to marry the likes of me?"

"I don't care what people say. If they have a problem with how people look that is their own problem, not ours. You aren't just a scarred face. You are a loving, living human so don't ever say you don't look like one."

"Rawhide, you have no idea how much you mean to me and how much happiness I feel when you tell me you love me. Are you absolutely sure you want to marry me though?"

She hugged him tighter. "Yes, and I will stand by your side forever and for always. I realized today that you are that person I have been waiting for, the one I truly love. The love I had for Johnny was sweet young love, but it was more like the infatuation a child. It had no comparison to the way I love you."

They finished the journey, hand in hand making plans for their future together. They would not announce their engagement until the big Christmas get together her mother was planning. Anicha, with husband and baby son were bringing Grandpa and Grandma Burak for a visit. It would be a perfect time. They would have their wedding the next day, while all the family was still together. Of course, they would include Frank and Eileen since they had been such a big part in her life.

When she got home that evening, she took Johnny's ring from around her neck, kissed it and put it in the box with his letters. She could not fall asleep for a long time that night, thinking of the peace she felt in her decision. She had finally found the person who she could spend the rest of her life with.

Richard spent a wakeful night as well. He was aware of the effect his presence had on most people. It was impossible not to know; the averted glances when people had to speak to him, backs quickly turned or gawking stares at his face. There were rude comments that hurt or being ignored as if he was an animal who could not speak. It had all hurt, but the biggest hurt was being sure he would never have a family of his own. Being here on this farm and working for Rawhide was the best he ever expected to have in life. Now, to have her tell him she loved him and wanted to be his forever was almost more than he could believe. However, it brought some other issues that he would have to address before they were married. Things she would have to know about, and It troubled him. Sleep eluded him that night in spite of his physical weariness.

CHAPTER 31

Rawhide was busy. There were three big trials coming up that she had to prepare for, and only a bit more than two months to plan for the wedding. She was glad that they had decided on a small wedding, otherwise she would have given up in despair.

Since it would be a family wedding she could have the reception in her own house and keep the foods simple and easy to serve. After announcing the engagement at Christmas time, she would ask Anicha to stand up with her. Richard said he would ask her husband, Dan.

Once they had the church booked and the pastor in agreement, almost everything was ready for their big day.

Whenever they were around her family, they did not let on that anything had changed between them. Even the boys did not suspect at first. With all the cooking and decorating, Robby finally found out, but he was sworn to secrecy and he promised not to tell anyone.

She had purchased her wedding dress, but Richard seemed adamant about not getting a suit. "What is wrong with just wearing my jeans?" he would ask each time she brought up the subject of a suit.

He and Robby were away one afternoon when she decided to take the matter of a suit into her own hands. If she measured a pair of his best fitting jeans and one of his shirts, she should be able to purchase a suit that would fit him.

The pair of jeans she wanted to measure lay on top of his bed. As she picked them up a metal tag dropped from the pocket to the floor. As she bent to retrieve it, she saw the name 'John Richard Carpenter', engraved in the metal, along with other pertinent information.

Every emotion possible raced through her. First there was a flash of pure joy that Johnny was alive. The joy was quickly replaced by anger. If Richard was Johnny, why had he deceived her and not told her who he was? If this person was indeed Johnny, why had he waited all these years to come home again?

"I am going to have to deal with this calmly," she told herself as confusion took the place of some of her anger. She realized she felt differently about Johnny than she did about Richard. It couldn't work for him to be both. Her mind would not accept that Johnny and Richard were the same person. Mixing love with anger has the same effect as mixing fire with gasoline. Within moments she was ready to explode. If Richard had walked in the door at that moment it would not have been a good scene.

Once her emotions calmed, her mind cleared. She was a lawyer, noted for finding every clue and getting to the bottom of things. Was this man she thought of as Richard, who had written his last name of Byldr, actually Johnny Carpenter? Or was he an imposter who knew that Johnny had wealth? It was not unheard of for a dog tag to be stolen from a dead soldier.

She remembered that just before her old farm manager left the farm he had told her that he and Richard had served in the air force together. He called him Richard, not Johnny! Was he part of some scheme too? And how did the manager know who he was? This man had no face and he could have said he was anybody.

She had never checked this Richard out for herself; never asked for his ID and had naively believed he was who he said he was without one question. This was so unlike her. She had a reputation of never being trapped in a legal battle because she followed every clue with tenacity. Had she let herself become entrapped in someone's scheme?

With the dog tag in hand she walked back to her house. If this person was John Richard Carpenter, he would have to prove it to her. So much for buying a suit for him! There would be no wedding without proof of his identity and some heavy-duty apologies!

Grasping for any clues to his real identity she thought of Frank. They had spent hours working together and if this person was his own son, they would have shared experiences from the past that only a father and his son could know. She was sure that Frank had no idea this person was masquerading as his only son. If it was Johnny and Frank and Eileen knew it, they would have said something to her. She and Johnny had many memories, but she had shared them with this Richard person, and he had only listened. He had shared nothing of mutual memories. This made her even more sure she had been duped by an imposter. If he had been Johnny, he could not have sat and listened while she talked about her love for him.

As soon as she was back in her house, she tried to phone Frank and Eileen, but there was no answer. The house was filled with all the decorations she had put up in preparation for the soon coming wedding reception. Stifling an urge to tear them all down she got out her baking bowls instead and mixed a large batch of bread. Not that she needed the bread, but punching dough was a way to work out her anger and confusion.

"I need to keep focused," she told herself. One of her favorite sayings as a lawyer was, "We need to listen to them before we hang them," meaning that everyone has a right to speak no matter how guilty they appear. "That," she decided, "is a good idea in principle. It does not work as well when it is one's own heart that is battered and possibly betrayed."

On a whim she went to her box of keepsakes, took out the ring and dog tag, as well as Johnny's last letter. Trudging down the icy path between the two houses she placed the items in the center of Richard's kitchen table. He couldn't miss it and he couldn't miss the message of the returned ring either.

Her anger cooled somewhat as she remembered all the kindness Richard or Johnny or whoever he was had showered her with. As she calmed down, she regretted putting the ring beside the dog tag. It was a rash act and she decided to get it again as soon as the bread was done baking.

She never got the chance. She had just pulled the last brown, crusty loaf from the oven when Robby burst into the house, loaded with packages and overflowing with good humor. Eager to share the adventures of his day, he quickly dumped his packages on his bed. Back in the kitchen he cut a thick crusty slice of bread and slathered it with butter. Mouth half full, he began, "Richard and I went to Grandpa and Grandpa Carpenter's house today. She said she has something special for me for Christmas, but she won't tell me what it is. All she would tell me is that it is too big to go under the tree. After that we went shopping and Richard got something to surprise you, but I can't tell you what it is. I know it will make you happy though."

Giving his mother a buttery kiss on her cheek he raced upstairs to his room.

CHAPTER 32

She was sitting by the cold fireplace with her head in her hands when he, Johnny, Richard, or whoever he was, came into the living room and sat on the rug beside her. The silence was long.

If his face could have shown expression, she would have seen the mixture of love and sorrow he was feeling.

"Who are you," she asked at last. "Remember Robby once told you if you were a bad man I would find out and send you to jail."

"You know now that I am Johnny as well as Richard," he responded softly. "You saw my name on the dog tag. What more can I say?"

She shook her head. "A name on a dog tag is not good enough for me. It could have been stolen. I need proof. I have told you all my memories with Johnny, so recalling them now is not going to work. You have to provide real and tangible proof before I will accept that you are John Richard Carpenter."

His voice was low as he spoke. "Rawhide, you have shared all those memories and sometimes I would cry myself to sleep, knowing how much you loved me, and I was so marred that I could never tell you who I am. There is one memory that will prove that I am who I say I am. He held up the ring she had taken to his house. "I gave you this ring and asked you to wear it around your neck. I had a matching one on a chain around my own neck. We were to wear these until I came home and then we would get married and place them on our fingers."

"I probably told you that," she said cooly. 'That is not proof."

"You did tell me," was his response. "but I still wear my ring. In fact, I will wear it for my entire life."

Shaking her head, she said, "That does not prove anything to me. You could have stolen it along with the dog tag."

He sighed. "For sure, someone can steal a ring and they probably did, because I don't have it anymore."

"You just told me you were still wearing your ring and now you tell me you don't have it. I do not appreciate falsehood and I have just caught you in one. This discussion is over!" She stood to leave the room but waited for his response.

He sighed. "Being interrogated by a lawyer is hard. Since my words are confusing you, let me give you tangible proof that I will always wear that ring." He stood and slowly unbuttoned his shirt. There, above his heart was the perfect brand of the ring. There was no mistaking that this brand, burned into his flesh, and the ring he held in his hand were identical. "The same fire that burned my face heated the ring and branded me. Is this tangible proof enough that I am the rightful owner of my own dog tag?" There was a touch of sarcasm in his voice. "If not, I also have Government issued identification in my name that I could show you. You could then contact someone in the Government to verify my identity."

There was another long silence between them. She knew she had hurt him by doubting him, she should apologize, but she wasn't finished yet. With a hint of the anger she still felt she said, "I will accept that brand as proof that you are the person you say you are, but I am not done yet. When were you planning to tell me you are Johnny? Were you going to spring that on me during the marriage ceremony when they use your full name and then hope I won't go hysterical in public?"

"Rawhide, the reason I had that dog tag out was that I was planning to very tenderly tell you tonight, in my own time and in my own way, that I am Johnny. I did not come home expecting to be in court with a lawyer interrogating me and doubting my honesty. I had planned a romantic evening and probably there would be lot of tears. I was prepared for that. I don't feel romantic right now. Instead, I pity the people you interrogate in real court sessions. How many of them do you make strip naked before you believe they have a legal right to their own names?" He stood. "I am going to build this fire before we talk more. I have a lot to tell you and it is very cold in here."

He soon had a roaring fire in the fireplace. As he sat down beside her, he chuckled a little. Do you still have your rawhide booties on? You were one tough little girl, and you have grown up to be one tough lady, my Little Rawhide!"

She ignored his comment and started to cry. "This has hurt me so much," she sobbed. "How could you go on pretending to be a man called Richard, when I kept talking about Johnny and how much I loved him. You are two completely different people to me now. I can't even think of you as Johnny. I am so confused right now. I am not sure I like either one of you, if that makes any sense." Angry, hurt tears were spilling down her flushed cheeks as she sat down in front of the fire.

"I did not intend to hurt you, my Little Rawhide. I am not making excuses when I say I don't know how I could have told you any sooner that I am Johnny. I was waiting for the perfect time and tonight was to be that night. It did not work out the way I planned. All I ask now is that you listen to why I never told you that I was Johnny. I was not trying to deceive you but to protect both our hearts from more pain than we have already gone through."

Richard sighed deeply. "Before I tell you anything though, I want to ask you two questions," he continued. "These are questions that you can only answer to yourself. This is the first question: If Johnny would have come home, how did you imagine him looking? The second question is this: When you picked up that marred and ugly derelict on the road that day, the one Robby called a bum, the one you could not look directly at,what would you have done if I had rushed up to you with open arms and told you I was Johnny? Just think about your own feelings."

Her face was a study of emotions as she thought of what her own feelings would have been.

He pulled her to her feet and led her to an easy chair before taking the chair beside her. "I hope by the time I am through you will understand why I did not come home when I was alive and why I never told you who I was when I did come back."

He arose and tucked a blanket around her before he began. "My plane was hit by enemy fire during the Battle of Pearl Harbor. Our instrument panel went dead and we were losing altitude fast. By some miracle our plane did not burst into flames immediately. I had to bring the plane down as we were losing all that fuel. We were over some mountainous area where there was no safe place to land but I tried to bring it down in the best place I could. I got it landed but it was a very rough landing. Everything exploded when we hit. I was blown from the plane with only my face and hands burned but I had a lot of broken bones. My buddy was trapped inside, calling for me to help him as the plane burned. I was fully conscious, but I was so broken I couldn't move to help him. It was so terrible, and I still have nightmares of him screaming my name and I am not able to move."

"In a war, not everyone is your enemy. Some people who lived there in the mountains found me and took me to their humble home, just a hut really. As I mentioned I had a lot of broken bones besides the burns on my face and hands. They carried me to someone who could set the bones and treat my burns, then cared for me as if I was their own son. I was starting to be able to get around again when I came down with some horrible sickness. This high fever kept returning every time I thought I was getting better. I was probably there for at least 5 years before I was well again. I didn't even know the war was over until I was well enough to come out of the mountain area."

Rawhide listened silently, her eyes wide, trying to imagine his pain.

"I wanted to come back to Canada, but I had no money for travel. If there was any Government help for me, a Canadian on US territory, I never found it. I tried to get a job of some kind, but for a long time no one would hire me. I finally found a job in a field, harvesting pineapples. They warned me that I was to work alone at the far end of the fields, so the other workers would not have to see my face. It didn't pay very much. I tried to get in touch with my parents to help me get back home, but the letter came back marked, "Return to Sender. Address Unknown." With them gone I had no one to help me come home. I contacted the legal office where I had my will, hoping there was money I could receive but I could not prove my identity in any way. There may have been a Canadian Consulate in Hawaii. If there was, I never located it, and no one would talk to me or answer my questions when I asked directions. Where ever it was, it was nowhere near where I was. I gave up and just kept working out there in the pineapples and wondering if this was how I would live for the rest of my life."

He stood, "That bread smells so good. May I have some? Thinking about the next few years makes me hungry." He rose to cut a thick slice. "You are the best cook, Rawhide. This is not flattery, it is the truth. You don't know how thankful I am for every bite of good food I eat."

"Anyway," he went on, "It took me three years of pulling pine-apple to have enough money to travel home. I was soon to learn that coming home was not as easy as buying a ticket and getting on a plane. All I had for identification was my dog tag. That is not a good form of identification. The person named on the tag was listed as MIA years before, so either I was a deserter who just decided to surface now when the war was long over, or I was an imposter who was try-ing to get into Canada with a stolen dog tag. Without facial features and my finger prints burned, I could not be easily identified. They took blood tests and I was placed in detention while they supposedly tried to figure out who I really was. I think I was lost in the system somewhere. I was there for at least another two years. They finally took another blood test and I was released shortly after that with an honorable discharge from the Airforce and also received a copy of my original birth certificate."

After getting a drink of water, he continued, "An honorable dis-charge did not get me a job. Everything had changed in the years I was gone. I tried to locate my parents again without success. There may have been some soldiers benefits I would have been eligible for, but since I had no fixed address, I was denied any help that might have been available."

"No one would hire me because my face was so burned and de-formed. I was hungry, and my clothes were ragged and more fitting for Hawaii than for Canada. It was a desperate time that pains me to even remember. I went to one home to beg for food and a drink of water. The woman wouldn't give me anything, instead she set her dogs on me. I got some nasty bites.

I probably would have died if I hadn't seen a poster advertising for a rodeo clown. I got the job although the committee that was hir-ing insisted that I would have to wear a mask, so I wouldn't frighten anyone or spook the horses. One of the men took me out for a good meal, the first full meal I had eaten for months, but he would not sit with me while I ate."

John Richard reached for Rawhides hand. I worked for the rodeo all that summer. I thought of you so often, Rawhide. I wanted to be who I used to be and come to you, but it couldn't be. I was alive but all my dreams of us were shattered. I knew by now that you would have inherited my land, but I could never come back as Johnny. I am broken, and I would not disrupt your life."

He saw her tears and his heart ached to take her in his arms, but he made no move to do so. "That winter was not as bad as healing from the plane crash, but it was a very close second. The only work I could find was cleaning out horse stables and it was not regular work. My clothing was too thin to keep out the cold and I had no blankets. I would crawl under hay at night to keep from freezing. I ate oats out of the horse's feed buckets and stole eggs from the neighbor's chicken house and ate them raw. It kept me alive. That is all I can say. When spring came, I went back to be a clown for the rodeo circuit, with my mask on to hide my missing face.

The rodeo organizers had booked a time to come here that summer. I was delighted because I would be able to see the land I had given you. I had no idea where you were living, but I hoped that I would be able to see you again without you ever finding out who I was. No matter what I was going through I had to know that my Little Rawhide was being cared for. I was walking down the road to this piece of land when you stopped and invited me to stay in your guest room. I knew who you were the minute you stopped your car.

I saw you had the farm built up almost the way I had dreamed of it being. I knew then that you still loved the old Johnny and I wished everything could be the way it was. I knew if I told you who I was you would take me back into your life immediately, but things would be forever changed. Love would be replaced with pity and a sense of obligation to me."

I never thought of staying on as your manager until my father and your former manager talked to me about it. Your manager and I knew each other in the Airforce. He may have told you that. My father had brought Alex out that day, never dreaming that I was here. When I told him who I was I was afraid he would never let go of me again. My father told your manager who I was. Your farm manager had actually been the General in charge of my unit.

After you came home from work that afternoon, I saw them walk over to your house and knew they were going to suggest you hire me. I wanted that job but I almost panicked when you asked me if I would work for you. To be able to live here and help you was a dream I had never dared to dream. I was so thankful for the job, and a home to live in without you knowing who I was. I could be close to you and be your friend and that would be as good as it could get.

"When we were children, I had been your protector Little Rawhide. When you hired me, you became my protector while I was still yours. When you asked me my name, I told you it was Richard, which is my second name. I was so thankful for a home and a job and I never planned to be anyone but "Richard". Once you asked me to sign my name and I signed it Richard Byldr. You fell in love with "Richard Byldr" because I was your friend and after a while you never wanted to part with me. You did not pity me or think you owed me a thing. What if you had known I was Johnny all along? I think you would have pitied me and cared for me, but I am no longer the boy you fell in love with. You would always feel beholden to Johnny. But could you have fallen in love with me if you had known who I really am?"

She rose and held out her hands to him. "I didn't understand. Thank you for opening my eyes with the questions you asked me. I feel so bad thinking of you out there half starved in the cold when everything here is yours, so, yes, I was actually pitying Johnny a lot as you were speaking. He should have come home to what was rightfully his. In fact, I feel a little angry that Johnny was so proud he couldn't come for what was his own. I feel terrible that you suffered so much though. Sorry if I sound like I am babbling. I am very confused right now. You are two different people in my mind."

She smiled up at him. "I am probably the first woman who has fallen in love with the same man with two different faces and two different names. Johnny was my first love. We were young and full of dreams. I always see his handsome, laughing face when I think of him. I have missed and mourned for that Johnny. You are so right. If he had not returned perfect, I would have had all this pity and could never have gotten past how he looked. He wouldn't be the same person, but I would still feel beholden to him for all he gave me."

"With you being Richard, it was just different. So thank you for not telling me at first. I have fallen deeply in love with you, just as you are and for who you are, without any pity. I owed you nothing. I treasure every scar on your funny face! That chilly evening when you put your coat around my shoulders, I realized I could never let you go out of my life."

"You will have to forgive me, but in my mind, you probably will never be Johnny. I have mourned for him and set him free. Our love was the innocence and passion of youth when one hasn't lived, suffered and still survived. You are the one my heart has loved with a mature love. You will always be Richard to me, the man I have chosen to marry and to love forever. I know I have told you all this before, but I need to repeat it again now that you have told me you are Johnny. I hope I am making sense but if I am not, be patient with me."

He stood and pulled her to his chest. "Does that mean I am forgiven then? If I am, I have a surprise or two for you." He brought in a huge bouquet of red roses along with the big box he had left in the entry. "The roses are from my heart to yours, no matter which one of me you love the most. The box is something I think will please you! Open it!"

She opened the box and lifted out a dark grey suit. "Richard! You got a suit after all? Oh, thank you!"

Soberly, he handed her the ring she had taken to his house that afternoon. "Johnny gave you this ring and as Johnny I am giving it back to you. As I showed you tonight, I will carry the brand of my ring above my heart, forever. Let's leave this ring as part of our old memories because neither of us are the same people we were as children. On our wedding day we will exchange new rings. I bought them today with Robby helping me choose them. I will leave them tucked in my dresser drawer until our big day." He paused. "By the way, what were you doing in my house anyway? Let me guess. You were going to buy me a suit? Am I right?"

She nodded. "I was going to measure your pants and the tag fell out."

"As I just said, we have both changed, Rawhide! The girl Johnny loved was this innocent little thing that had to be protected from bullies. She wore little rawhide booties to school and she was really cute. He loved her with all his young heart even though he was too young to know what real love is. The woman I now love is this beautiful lawyer, as tough as rawhide and can make a legal case out of a dog tag that she shouldn't have found in the first place! May I never have to face you in a real court on real charges! I think the person you have become would be far too tough for young Johnny but scarred and battered old Richard loves you just the way you are!"

She went to the kitchen and made them each a sandwich from the soft new bread and brought them back to where they were sitting in front of the fire. "I have had a lot of things to work through in my life," she said with a smile. "But this is by far the craziest. It has made me happy, but it is still crazy. If I go around looking confused for the rest of my life don't be surprised. I am not sure I will ever get my mind around all of this!"

He rose to leave and as she walked him to the door, he wrapped her in a giant bear hug. "Whoever I am in your mind, it is good to be home again with you, my Little Rawhide."

A few minutes later he popped his head in the door chuckling. "I was just wondering. Does Johnny get his farm back and share it with you, or does Richard have to work for you for the rest of his life?"

She stepped out and scooped up a handful of fluffy snow and tossed it at him. "Guess that is something we are just going to have to work out between the three of us." she laughed as she closed the door.

CHAPTER 33

Christmas festivities began on Christmas eve at the Romanov household. It was a night of feasting and fun. Richard, with Anicha's husband and the boys spent some time tobogganing down the hills, coming in covered with snow and frost. Peter, who had grown a huge bushy beard was dubbed Santa, and Anicha's little boy sat on his knee and asked him for the all the things he wanted. Santa promised him (in Russian) that all his dreams would come true but maybe he would have to work hard and wait most of his life for this to happen. The little boy smiled, having understood nothing.

Quiet Dr. Anicha helped her mother, sister and niece in the kitchen, getting everything ready for tomorrows feast. Olena cried at the sight of all the food. She would never forget the terrible famine and seeing her peasant friends dying, one by one, of starvation, or the people in the Nazi slave labor camps dying of hunger and exhaustion. She would carry those sights, sounds and fear with her to her grave.

When everyone was quiet, Nataliya pulled her own parents, Ivan and Olena, from their easy chairs and sat them on kitchen chairs in the middle of the room. "Anicha and I were there with our mother, Olena. We know the life we led in the little village. We grew up knowing our father had been taken at gunpoint. Olena never knew what happened to him but, she always filled us with faith that he had survived. Quite by accident I found him. Although I know his story, it has not been told to the others. My father, how did you get to Canada way back then?"

Ivan smiled. "My story isn't so long. The soldiers had their guns in my back, marching me toward whatever was waiting as my fate. Two big dogs jumped out of the darkness and attacked the soldiers. We were walking by a high fence and it gave me a moment to jump over that fence. I knew where I was and where I was going. They didn't.

By the time they had dealt with the dogs they could no longer find me. I made it to the road and met up with the man with the load of hay. Everything went as planned except my wife and girls were not there. I had no idea where they were, and it was too dangerous to look for them. I had to leave but my heart was breaking. When I found Nataliya, I was so happy to find my daughter. When Anicha came, I was doubly blessed, but I still had no idea where my Olena was. When Olena and I were finally together after all those years, my life did start over again. Our family is very blessed. We have all found each other again. There are not many happy stories like ours, so our thankfulness is very great."

It was a joyful, warm time of family togetherness, in spite of the cold outside. Olena and Ivan Burak beamed at the little dynasty they had created. Their lives were almost over but they found joy in family togetherness. Their lives had been spent alone for too long and this family time was more joyful for them than any of the younger ones would ever comprehend. They were getting feeble and no longer liked to travel. This would probably be the last time they could all be together this way. They were showered with love and attention by the three generations of their descendants.

After a short rest, Peter and Alex sang a song in a tongue that only Ivan and Olena had heard before, the language of the Roma. The melody was haunting. Olena understood enough to know it was a love song written by Peter himself for Nataliya that told of their young dreams.

When the song was done, he seated himself beside his Mother-in Law and smiled down at her. "Yes, I now confess to you, Mother Olena. My father was Roma. My mother was Russian, so I have my mother's last name. I grew up very rich and pampered until the Revolution. My mother grew up almost like a Princess, but my father was a gypsy musician, that loved and left my mother. So you were half right. The heart of your lovely daughter was stolen away by a gypsy, just like you thought."

Olena patted his arm and smiled. "Somehow, that is not important to me anymore. Maybe you can forgive me for hating you so much? I confess I did hope your ship would sink on the way to Canada, so I could be done with you. Now, in spite of everything you and Nataliya have been through, I am so thankful you got her out of the Ukraine when you did.

He laughed his hearty laugh. "I can forgive you, of course, and I want to thank you for this beautiful daughter you raised. Nataliya's strength and courage brought us through a lot of hard times. She got that strength from you as, has our own daughter, Rawhide."

The next day was another day of feasting and merriment along with sharing gifts and memories. Eileen led Robby to the old pole barn for his gift of the very large St. Bernard pup that he had begged for. He insisted on bringing the pup in the house and spent much of the day trying to keep it from howling. Eventually, he borrowed the car and took his dog home, returning in time for more feasting and fun.

****

At last the house grew quiet. Rawhide walked to the center of the room. "You all know that Johnny Carpenter was the love of my young life. He never came back from the war but left me a legacy that has helped our family and many others to have a better life. That gift was greatly appreciated, but I could have made myself a good life without it because of a far better gift he gave me. He gave me that gift on the first day of school when I was being hurt and bullied by the other children. I was dressed in rags and had rawhide booties on my feet. One child knocked me face down in the dirt. Johnny picked me up and wiped the blood off my face, then shared his lunch with me. The children called me 'Baby Bohunk,' 'Rawhide,' and 'Cattle Thief'. That is when Johnny gave me the greatest gift anyone can give a child. He accepted me just as I was, to be his friend. He told me to be proud of the name Rawhide because I was tough, like Rawhide. His love for me and his faith in me brought me through some hard times long after he was gone. Because someone believed in me and loved me, I grew up believing I was an OK person and could make it through hard times."

She paused. "Johnny went MIA in the battle of Pearl Harbor. I never stopped grieving for him and I am not sure how I would have managed if his parents had not stepped in. They gave me an unbelievable amount of moral support and help with the cattle and the little boys, plus they encouraged me and gave me an education. I owe so much to Frank and Eileen. When you look at me, you see a successful lawyer, but I did not get there on my own. I got there from the help of people who cared about me and believed in me. Aunt Anicha asked me just yesterday why I am not married," she smiled. "The real reason has been that I could never find anyone I could love as much or more than Johnny. I chose tonight to share with all of you that I am going to get married. I found someone who I want to be with for the rest of my life. This person is special to me in a way Johnny never was."

At the shouts of, "Tell us who?" she began to sing, "Whither thou goest I will go."

Richard walked to her. She faced him, placed her hands above his heart and sang, "Wherever thou lodgest, I will lodge." They heard the gasps from the family members seated near them

"Thy people shall be my people, my love." As she sang these words, Frank and Eileen circled the two younger people in their arms.

She sang on, "For, as in that story, long ago, the same sweet love story now is so."

She stopped and looked at Frank who cleared his throat and wiped at some tears. "You all know that our son did not return from the war." He began. "He was my only child. I think the only way Eileen and I survived our grief was by helping this very special young lady. She was all we had left of our Johnny."

"We are very proud of her, by the way," interrupted Eileen, giving Rawhide a little squeeze.

"You all know what Rawhide is like," Frank went on. "She was always bringing people who were down and out to her guest house, giving them a few good meals and courage to go out and face their world again. It was no surprise to anyone when she picked up a ragged, scarred man one day and brought him to her barn guest house. I happened to come for a visit while he was there, and within a short time realized that this man you all know as Richard, is my son Johnny. He made me promise never to tell Rawhide who he was as he did not want her pity or have her feel she owed him anything."

It was Richard's turn to speak. "My father talked her in to hiring me as her farm manager. I assumed I would have this job forever, but it was hard being with the girl I had loved all my life and never be able to tell her who I was. Like my father said, I did not want her pity. But she fell in love with me, ugly as I am. She tells me Johnny was her girlhood crush, but I am the love of her life. She says she can't think of me as anyone but Richard. As Johnny, I promised my little Rawhide I would always take care of her. As Richard, I will always treasure this strong woman. We will walk together hand in hand for as long as we live and take care of each other. We are getting married tomorrow at two in the afternoon. We want you all there at our wedding."

The room erupted in shouts, tears, cheers and clapping as they circled the couple.

She talked privately to her parents later that evening and explained to them that because of the past she did not wish her father to walk her down the aisle, or her parents to give her away. "I want you to know you are forgiven for the past, but this marriage is my own choice. But I would like it if you would stand and sing as I walk down the aisle." She knew her words saddened them, but they assured her they understood

The wedding was beautiful and touching. Dressed in a simple white silk dress that featured a long flowing cape of soft white velvet, her dark curls caught in a band on top of her head and flowing loosely down her back, she was the picture of loveliness. In her hands she carried the old worn Bible that had belonged to Eileen's mother.

She walked alone to where John Richard Carpenter waited to lead her to the altar and claim Rawhide, the only girl he had ever loved, as his wife.

They came out of the church to a winter wonderland. Snow was falling heavily in large feathery flakes, hiding the scarred earth of the roadway and all the old crusted snow under a snowy blanket of beauty that covered every imperfection. "The snow is like our love that has covered all our scars and pain under a cloak of beauty," she said softly.

He took her hand as they stepped into the deep snow together. Their love had lasted and grown richer through their long, painful and separate journeys. His heart was bursting with the joy of it as he whispered, "My Little Rawhide. I promise I will be with you for as long as we live."

POSTLUDE

Rawhide rose gracefully as she collected our teacups on our last evening together. "Now you know much of our story. I know you are going to ask why Johnny never had plastic surgery. He did and something went terribly wrong. He got a severe infection and, in the end,, he was more scarred than he had been before. Some things just are what they are and we move on," she said gently as she pointed to the photo of a handsome young man. "This was Johnny before the war and you met Richard in the home! I never could quite convince myself they were the same person and I am sure you can understand why!"

"The kindness that Johnny showed me as a little child and again later, touched many more lives than just my own. The pain and stigma of race prejudice and false accusations were healed because of that gift and the injured ones were able to lift up their heads and become the people they really were. In turn, they helped others. The money meant little, in comparison to the gift of kindness and acceptance.

His gift even touched his own life in the bizarre twist that life sometimes makes. It provided a home, friendships, and a job for himself until I fell in love with Richard and learned he was Johnny. It went the full circle."

I thanked her for sharing her own story and the stories of her people with me as I rose to go. I needed to go home that night and went to my room for my suitcase. As I carried it to the car, I knew I would miss her and this time we had spent together. There was something about her that made me feel welcome and at ease, rather than a stranger invading her home and her memories.

She walked to the car with me and as we said our 'Goodbyes', she gently touched my arm. "Always remember from now on that every person you meet has their own story to tell and not all of them are happy ones. Your acts of kindness can bring hope to the struggling and hurting ones. You may hold their future and the future of their children in your hands and on your tongue. Never forget the power of caring! You are more powerful than you think!" She handed me a tiny envelope. "There are some very important words inside. Be sure to read them!"

I nosed my car down the narrow mountain road. There had been a snowfall, and the moonlight reflecting from the snowy mountains turned the world into a night sparkling with jewels and gold. My mind was not on the beauty around me however, but on the beautiful character of Rawhide.

She had spent her childhood in extreme poverty and hard work while living with her ill and depressed parents. Those same parents selfishly betrayed her. She was raped, forced into a loveless marriage and abused. The boy that she did love went MIA and one can only imagine her grief since he was the one person she could depend on. At the age of sixteen she gave birth and had her own child and an invalid baby brother to care for. Just when she had the means to make a change in her life, the herd of cattle she planned to sell were taken from her. She faced all of this during her childhood and teen years. In that period in history, children had no voice or legal protection from this type of treatment. Many children who faced far less than she had broke down and spent the rest of their lives in asylums for the insane, as they were called. Others took their own lives, feeling there was no way out of the chaos they were in.

Somehow, out of her own personal suffering she became compassionate instead of bitter. She understood the pain of others and chose to devote her life to giving a voice and hope to the hurting and disadvantaged with unparalleled empathy. My question was how could so much love come from a person who had been so injured herself?

I came to a pullout in the highway and stopped to take in the beauty of the night. Below me, a river still open, meandered; a glistening line of silver through its snowy banks. The evergreen branches were heavy with snow and above me the white mantle covering the mountains glistened in the brightness from the light of the full moon shining down on the scene. I opened the envelope she gave me and read the words she had penned. "These three remain: faith, hope and love, but the greatest of these is love. Corinthians 13:13."

Understanding came as I stood there. The moonlight that was making the night beautiful was the sunlight being reflected. No matter how many storms there are on the moon, it still shines.

That is when I realized that the strength to pick up her life and go on, the inner beauty that Rawhide exuded, came from someone seeing her worth just the way she was. Protected from bullying, admired, loved and included as a child in school, she developed strength to survive a less than ideal childhood. As a teen victim of severe trauma, loving communication and physical help from her former fiancé's parents kept her moving forward. The love given to her by Johnny and his parents was like the sun. The beauty of her character developed from a reflection of the love she had received. She in turn had shone that love for others.

Many years have passed but I will never forget the woman they called Rawhide.